'Will you, Sop[...] with me in La [...]

There was a heartbeat of a pause while she considered the alternative. 'I will,' she said in a low voice, thinking with a poignant longing how much like a wedding vow that sounded. But he was not offering her marriage. He wanted her, yes, and he was entrusting her with the care of his son. But not love. Not marriage.

His mistress and his son's carer.

'You would leave all this behind?' he asked.

'I would.'

'Why?'

'Because of your son,' she faltered, and saw his face suddenly became shuttered.

'And…and for you, Luis.'

'But why for me, exactly, *querida*?' he questioned softly.

'I want you.'

Sharon Kendrick started story-telling at the age of eleven and has never really stopped. She likes to write fast-paced, feel-good romances with heroes who are so sexy they'll make your toes curl!

Born in west London, she now lives in the beautiful city of Winchester—where she can see the cathedral from her window (but only if she stands on tiptoe). She is married to a medical professor—which may explain why her family get more colds than anyone else on the street—and they have two children, Celia and Patrick. Her passions include music, books, cooking and eating—and drifting off into wonderful daydreams while she works out new plots!

Recent titles by the same author:

PROMISED TO THE SHEIKH
  (*Society Weddings* 2-in-1 short story)
THE MISTRESS'S CHILD
THE SICILIAN'S PASSION

MISTRESS OF LA RIOJA

BY

SHARON KENDRICK

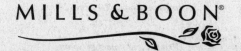

MILLS & BOON®

For my darling TK, who has inspired more
passion and romance than he will ever know…

*MILLS & BOON and MILLS & BOON with the Rose Device
are registered trademarks of the publisher.*

*First published in Great Britain 2002
Harlequin Mills & Boon Limited,
Eton House, 18-24 Paradise Road, Richmond, Surrey TW9 1SR*

© Sharon Kendrick 2002

ISBN 0 263 82947 2

*Set in Times Roman 10½ on 12¼ pt.
01-0702-44264*

*Printed and bound in Spain
by Litografia Rosés, S.A., Barcelona*

CHAPTER ONE

THE phone chose precisely the wrong moment to ring. Up to her eyes in spreadsheets, Sophie gave a little groan of irritation as she clicked the button up. She still had masses to get through, which was why she had been in the office since the crack of dawn.

She normally worked from around eight until late—however late she needed to be to get the job done; no one could ever accuse Sophie of a lack of dedication, but for once she wanted to leave early. To spend an outrageously indolent time getting ready for a date. A hot date, too—with Oliver Duncan, owner of rival ad agency Duncan's.

She wriggled her shoulders with anticipation—because she was about to spend the evening with one of London's most eligible men and was currently the envy of all her single girlfriends!

'Now, I *did* say I didn't want to be disturbed, Narell,' she joked in mock-stern tone, knowing full well that Narell was the best assistant in the world, so maybe it was important. It had better be!

But Narell's voice sounded strained. 'I'm afraid that this man wouldn't take no for an answer. He insisted he speak to you.'

Sophie pulled a face.

'Insisted, did he?' she mused aloud. 'I'm not sure I like men who insist! Who is it?'

'It's…it's…' Narell cleared her throat, as if she

couldn't quite believe the name she was saying. 'It's
Don Luis de la Camara.'

Luis.

Luis!

Sophie gripped the desk as if holding on to it for
dear life. How mad, how crazy—that just the mention
of his name was enough to bring her out into a cold
sweat.

She felt excitement. Gut-wrenching and stomach-
melting excitement. And then, hard on the heels of
excitement came guilt. She felt its icy heat pin-
pricking at her brow.

Just what was it about Luis de la Camara? She
knew what kind of man he was. Shallow and sexy
and completely out of bounds, and yet here she was
now, calm and rational Sophie—Sophie who was supposed to be excited at the thought of dating Oliver—
only now her heart was racing like a speeding train
as she stared at the phone. Oliver was forgotten, and
in his place exploded the dark presence of the most
formidable man she had ever met.

But she pulled herself together, wondering why the
arrogant Spaniard was ringing her here, at work, and
demanding to speak to her, no less!

Ruing the day that her cousin had ever married
him, Sophie gave a reluctant nod. 'OK, Narell. You
can put him through.'

'Right.'

There was a momentary pause and then Sophie
heard the unmistakable voice of Luis de la Camara,
pouring like rich, sensual honey down through the
intercom, and despite her good intentions she felt the
slow wash of awareness creeping colour across her

pale cheeks. He's married, she reminded herself, and he's married to your cousin. A man you despise, remember?

But animosity was an acquired skill she had learned along the way. She had had to teach herself to hate him. Far better to hate a man than to admit that he excited you in a way which was as frightening as it was inappropriate. And how could you feel anything other than hate for a man who could look at a woman with pure, undiluted lust in his eyes—just days before he was due to be married to her cousin?

'Soph-ie?'

He said her name as no one else did. The slight lilt to the voice, the faintest idiomatic Spanish accent which could send goosebumps all over your skin. She hastily clicked the switch down and grabbed the receiver—the last thing she wanted was the amplification of those dark, richly accented tones filling her office.

'This is she,' she answered crisply. She put her pen down. 'Well, this is certainly a surprise, Luis.' And how was that for understatement?

'Yes.'

His voice sounded unfamiliar. Heavy. Hard. Burdened. And Sophie suddenly felt some ghastly premonition shiver its way over her skin as logic replaced her first instinctive reaction to hearing him. Her voice rose in fright. 'What's happened? Why are you ringing me at work?'

There was a moment of silence which only increased her foreboding, because Sophie had never heard Luis hesitate before. Indecision was not on his agenda. Some men were never at a loss for words and de la Camara was a prime example.

'What is it?' she whispered. 'What's wrong?'

'Are you sitting down?'

'Yes! Luis, for God's sake—*tell* me!'

In another world, another country away, Luis flinched. There was no easy way to say it, nothing he could do to ease the painful words. 'It's Miranda,' he began slowly. 'I am afraid to have to tell you, Sophie, that there has been a terrible accident. Your cousin…she has been killed. *Murió en un accidente de coche,*' he finished on a note of disbelief, as if only repeating the words in his native tongue could make him believe the terrible truth himself.

A cry was torn from Sophie's throat, so that she sounded like a wounded animal. 'No!'

'It is true,' he said.

'She's dead? Miranda is dead?' she questioned, as if, even now, he still had the opportunity to deny it. To make it go away.

'*Sí.* I am sorry, Soph-ie. So very sorry.'

Buffeting against the sick feeling in her stomach, the words punched their way home.

Dead! Miranda dead? 'But she can't be dead!' Sophie whimpered. How could a beautiful woman of twenty-five be no more? 'Say it isn't true, Luis.'

'Do you not think that if I could I would?' he said, and his deep voice sounded almost gentle as he carried on with the grim story. 'She died in a car crash earlier today.'

'No.' She shuddered, and closed her eyes.

Until an even more horrific scenario reared its terrifying head and they snapped open again. 'What

about Teodoro?' she cried, her heart clenching with
fear as she thought about her adorable little nephew.
'He—he wasn't with her, was he?'

'In the early hours of the morning?' he questioned
heavily. 'No, Sophie, he was not with her. My son
was tucked up in bed, safely asleep.'

'Oh, thank God!' she breathed, and, just as a great
wave of grief pierced her like a dagger, so did his
words imprint themselves on her consciousness.

If Teodoro was tucked up safely in bed, then what
was Miranda doing out in the early hours of the morning—and how come Luis had not been injured?
Unless…unless he *had* been injured. 'Were you hurt
yourself, Luis?' she questioned unsteadily.

In the fan-cooled air of the vast hacienda, Luis's
hard, dark features set themselves into bleak and unforgiving lines. 'I was not in the car,' he said roughly.

Though her thoughts were fragmented by the enor-
mity of what he had told her, Sophie frowned in confusion. Why not? she wondered. Why was Miranda
travelling in the early hours without her family?

Her fingers clenched themselves into a tight little
fist. The whys and the wheres and the hows were not
appropriate—not now, not when the cold practicali-
ties of death must be dealt with in as sympathetic a
way as possible.

And Luis must be grieving—he must be. Despite
the ups and downs of a marriage which Sophie knew
had definitely not been made in heaven. His wife—
the mother of his son—had met a tragically early end,
and, no matter what had gone on before, Luis's world
had imploded.

Her own feelings about him didn't count—not at a

time like this. He was owed her condolences and not her hostility.

'I'm...I'm so sorry,' she said stiffly.

'Thank you,' he said, his voice flat. 'I rang to tell you the news myself rather than having the police contact you. And to enquire whether you wish me to ring your grandmother...'

His words reminded her of the awful task which lay ahead—of telling her elderly and now frail grandmother what had happened. Sophie drew in a painful breath, thankful that her cousin's parents had been spared the ordeal of learning the fate of their beautiful daughter. For wasn't the premature death of a child the most terrible bereavement of all—even if they *had* treated Miranda with a kind of absent carelessness?

Miranda's parents had been nomads at heart, inveterate travellers who had journeyed to all four corners of the earth, greedily seeking out new experiences, never growing tired of the adventure of the unexplored. Until one day when their light aircraft had plummeted out of the sky and into the unforgiving mountains. Miranda had been just seventeen at the time, and soon after that, she had begun to live as though there were no tomorrow.

And now there never would be, not for her.

'No.' Biting back her tears, Sophie slowly let the word out. 'I will tell my grandmother myself, in person. It'll be easier...' She swallowed. She wouldn't break down in front of him, she wouldn't. 'Less painful, coming from me.' And try somehow to contact her own parents, who were having their own holiday of a lifetime, ensconced in luxury on some vast, ocean-going liner.

'You're sure?' he questioned.

'Yes.'

'It will be…hard,' he said, but his voice was un-characteristically soft now, soft as butter. 'She is an old woman now.'

She steeled herself not to react to that murmuring voice, because it was vital that she remained impervious to Luis de la Camara—for all their sakes. 'It is thoughtful of you to care.'

Did she mock him with that cool, unfathomable tone of hers? 'Of course. She is family, Sophie—what did you expect?'

What *did* she expect? She didn't know, and she wondered how he could ask her a question like that at a time like this.

She hadn't expected her beloved Miranda to die so needlessly, or for her nephew to grow up without a mother, so far away from the land of her birth.

Teo.

Just the thought of him focused Sophie's grief into energy and resolution. 'Wh-when is the funeral?'

'On Monday.'

Which gave her three days.

'I'll be there. I'll fly out on Sunday.'

And, to Luis's appalled horror, he felt the stirring of triumph and the impossible ache of knowing that soon he would see her once more, and he cursed the body which betrayed him so completely. 'Contact my home or my office to let me know the times of your flight,' he said tightly. 'You will have to fly to Madrid and then take a connection on to Pamplona. I will arrange to have a car pick you up at the airport. Have you got that?'

'Thank you,' she said, thinking how in control he sounded, until she remembered that he was in control—always—and that, whatever happened, it was Luis de la Camara who was calling the shots.

'*Adios,* Sophie,' he drawled softly.

With a shaking hand, Sophie let the phone fall down into its cradle, and at the harsh finality of the sound reaction set in at last. She stared blankly at the wall in front of her, her mind spinning with disbelief as she thought of Miranda.

Her poor cousin—dying alone in a strange, foreign country! Poor, sweet Miranda—envied by so many women, solely because she was married to a man so universally desired. A man whose child she had borne, whose money she had enjoyed, but whose heart had always been tantalisingly locked away from her.

A man, moreover, whose black eyes glittered with such stark sexual promise that Sophie could not imagine that he would have been able to remain faithful for even the first year of marriage.

After all, *she* had ignored the unmistakable invitation she had read there, but that was because she loved Miranda. She doubted whether other women would have such scrupulous morals where Luis de la Camara was concerned.

And now a little baby would now have to grow up without a mother.

Sophie's gaze was drawn to the silver-framed photo which stood in pride of place on her desk and she picked it up and studied it.

It showed Teodoro and it had been taken just before his first birthday, only a few short weeks ago.

He was an adorable child, but Teodoro's looks owed very little to her cousin's exquisite blonde beauty. Instead his face was stamped with the magnificent dominance of his father's colouring, and as she stared at it the image of his hard and handsome face came flooding back into her mind with bitter clarity.

Gleaming black eyes, fringed with sinfully thick lashes and hair which was as dark as the moonless night she had first met him. When she had virtually bumped into him in the deli at the end of her road and he had stopped dead, stared at her intensely, as if he knew her from somewhere, as if he couldn't quite believe his eyes.

And the feeling had been mutual. When just for a moment her heart had leapt with a wild and unexpected joy. And an unmistakable lust which had set up a slow, sweet aching.

The kind of thing which wasn't supposed to happen to sensible city girls who were cool and calm in matters of the heart.

Was it possible to fall in love in a split-second? she remembered helplessly thinking as she gazed at the proud, aristocratic features she seemed to have spent her whole life waiting for.

She'd seen his eyes darken, the heated flare of awareness which moved along the angular curve of his high cheekbones. His lush lips had unconsciously parted and she'd seen a thoroughly instinctive movement as his tongue flicked through to moisten them, and outrageously she had imagined that tongue on her body…in her body…

She had never been looked at with quite such insolent and arrogant appraisal before. He wants me, she'd thought, with the warm flooding of awareness. And I want him, too. She had found herself wondering whether she would be able to resist him if he touched her, while at the same time asking if she had completely taken leave of her senses.

And then Miranda had appeared, carrying a bottle of champagne, her mouth falling open in surprise. 'Sophie! Good heavens!' she exclaimed, and glanced up at him, not seeming to notice the brittle tension in the air which surrounded them. 'What an amazing coincidence! We were just on our way to see you, weren't we, darling?'

Darling?

With a jolt which went deeper than disappointment, Sophie registered dully that Miranda was possessively touching the arm of the tall, dark man with the glittering eyes and the softly gleaming lips. And the champagne...

'Are you—are you celebrating something?' she questioned with a sinking heart as she quickly realised exactly what they must be celebrating.

'We sure are! Sophie—I'd like to introduce you to Don Luis de la Camara,' Miranda announced proudly and then smiled up into the dark, shuttered face. 'Luis—this is my cousin, Sophie Mills.'

'Your cousin?' he questioned with a frown, and his voice was as rich and dark as bitter chocolate. The predatory look had disappeared in an instant, and Sophie had seen the rueful shrug which replaced it, knowing that Don Luis de la Camara would never look at her in that way again. As the cousin of his wife-to-be, she was much too close to home to play around with. But a man who looked like that just days

before his wedding *would* play around. Sophie recognised that with a blinding certainty and she hated
him for it.

'Well, we spent all our holidays together—so we're
more like sisters, really!' Miranda smiled her wide,
infectious smile. 'Sophie—we're getting married!
Isn't it wonderful? Luis has asked me to marry him!'

Sophie shuddered as she remembered the jealousy
which had ripped through her. To be jealous of your
own cousin! But she had forced a smile and hugged
Miranda and given Luis her hand, all too aware of
the warm tingle as their flesh touched. And he had
bent and raised her fingertips to his mouth, in an old-
fashioned and courtly style—faithful to the manner of
the Spanish aristocrat he was, his black eyes seeming
to mock and to tantalise her in tandem.

They had gone back to her flat and drunk champagne and chinked glasses and toasted the future. But
while Miranda had fizzed with life the Spaniard had
sat watchfully, choosing his words with care, looking
so right and yet so wrong in Sophie's flat and her
world. Because he was Miranda's, she had reminded
herself. Miranda's.

With an effort she pushed away the disturbing
memories and forced herself back to the present.
Concentrating on the image of the child in the photo
instead of the potent sexuality of his father.

At least Teodoro's face still had the softness of
innocence and she could see little of the indomitable
nature which so defined Luis.

She wondered what would happen to Teodoro
now—whether his mother's memory would be allowed to fade until it was so distant that it was almost

forgotten. Sophie bit her lip. What chance would he have of learning about his mother and the land of his mother's birth?

And suddenly a sense of duty dulled some of the raw edge of sorrow. Luis shall not take him from us entirely, she vowed. I will fight for the opportunity to get to know him as if he were my own! And he will know me, too. With a trembling hand, she buzzed through to Narell to ask her to book her flight to Spain.

And then she washed her face, dragged a comb through her hair and called Liam Hollingsworth into the office, who took one look at her and started.

'What the hell have you been doing to yourself?' he demanded. 'Are you OK?'

Her voice still trembling slightly, she said, 'Not really, no.'

'For God's sake, Sophie—what's the matter? What's happened to you?'

She framed the unbelievable words. 'It's my cousin, Miranda,' she told him. 'She's been…killed in an accident. I've…I've got to go and break the news to my grandmother—'

'Oh, my God.'

'And th-then fly on to Spain to the funeral.'

'Oh, honey!' He was round her side of the desk in an instant, staring down at her with a look of dazed concern on his face as she began to cry. 'Honey!'

'Oh, Liam!' she sobbed.

'Come here,' he said gently, and put his arms around her.

She allowed herself to cry a little more, but after a couple of moments she broke away and went to stand by the window, staring out at a world which no longer looked the same place. 'I still can't believe it,' she said dully.

'What happened?' he asked.

'I know very few facts. Just that she was in a car crash. I was too…too shocked to ask for any details, I guess.'

'How did you find out?'

'Her husband, Luis—he rang me from Spain to tell me.'

He frowned. 'That's the millionaire guy—the one you can't stand?'

'That's the one,' she said tightly, thinking how much more complex the truth was than a simple case of not being able to stand the man.

'And when's the funeral?'

'Monday. I'm flying out on Sunday.' She sighed. 'Oh, Liam, I don't know if I can bear it.'

He nodded understandingly. 'Well, it'll be hard, but at least after that you need never meet again.'

Sophie shook her head. 'But it isn't that easy. I wish it was. I can't just spirit Luis out of my life, however much I might want to. Don't forget—he's the father of my nephew, and I feel I owe it to Miranda, and to *Teodoro*…' The words seemed to come from an unknown place deep inside her. 'To fight for him.'

Liam stared at her. 'Fight for him?' he echoed. 'You surely don't mean you're going to apply for custody, Sophie? You wouldn't stand a hope in hell. Not if he's as rich and as powerful as you say he is. And he *is* the father.'

Tiredly, Sophie rubbed at her temples. 'I don't know what I mean—other than knowing I have to get out there. To let Teo know that he has relatives, and that we care.'

'And once the funeral is over? Will you come straight back?'

She met his eyes. 'I don't know. I can't commit to a time scale. But I'll still be able to do *some* work— I can always use my laptop, and you'll be able to manage here without me for a bit, won't you?'

'Of course we can manage,' he said quietly. 'We'll just miss you, that's all.'

'Thanks,' she whispered, and, gulping back more tears, she began to pack her briefcase.

She and Liam went way back.

They had met at university and discovered a shared sense of humour coupled with an ambition to make lots of money while having *fun*. Which had been how the Hollingsworth-Mills advertising agency had come about. Now they were tipped for the top. A combination of enthusiasm and employing bright young staff with similar high-reaching goals meant that Sophie and Liam were poised on the brink of unforeseen success.

But what did any of that matter at a time like this?

Feeling too shaky to drive safely, she took the train to Norfolk, her heart weeping for her grandmother as she walked up the path of her Norfolk country cottage, where she and Miranda had spent part of their school holidays, every summer without fail. They had walked for miles on the vast, empty beaches which were close by, and climbed trees and fed the fat ducks on the pond with pieces of bread.

And Sophie had watched as Miranda's beauty had become something more than breathtaking. Had seen for herself the bewitching power which that beauty gave her over men...

She rang the old-fashioned jingly-jangly doorbell, praying for the right words to tell her grandmother what had happened, and knowing that there were none which would not hurt.

But Felicity Mills was almost eighty, and there was little of life she hadn't seen. She took one look at Sophie's face. 'It's bad news,' she said flatly.

'Yes. It's Miranda—'

'She's dead,' said her grandmother woodenly. 'Isn't she?'

'How? How could you possibly have known that?' Sophie whispered, much later, when tears had been shed and they had sought some kind of comfort in old photographs of Miranda as a baby, then a sunny toddler and every other stage through to stunning bride. But Sophie hadn't wanted to linger on *that* photo—not when the dark face of Luis mocked her and stung her guilty conscience. 'How?' she asked again.

'I can't explain it,' sighed her grandmother. 'I just looked into your face and I knew. And, in a way, there was a dreadful inevitability about it. Miranda always flew too close to the sun. One day she was bound to get burned.'

'But how can you be so *accepting?*'

'How can I not? I have lived through war, my darling. You have to accept what you cannot change.'

She squeezed the old woman's hand. 'Is there—is there anything I can do for you, Granny?'

There was a long silence and Mrs Mills stared at her. 'There is one thing—but it may not be possible.

I'm too old and too frail to fly to Spain for the funeral—but I should like to see Teodoro again before I die.'

Sophie swallowed down the lump in her throat. Surely that wasn't too much to ask—even of Luis—not under these circumstances. 'Then I'll br-bring him to you,' she promised shakily. 'I promise.'

'But Luis might not allow it.'

Sophie's eyes glimmered with unshed tears. 'He must, Granny—he *must!*'

'It is a big favour to ask him. Tread carefully, Sophie—you know how fiercely possessive he is about his son and you know the kind of man you're dealing with,' her grandmother added drily. 'You know his reputation. Few would dare to cross him.'

'I'm hoping it won't come to that,' said Sophie, then stared up at her grandmother, her eyes confused. 'Don't you hate him, Granny? For making Miranda so unhappy?'

'Happiness is not the gift of one person to another,' answered her grandmother slowly. 'It takes two people to be happy. And hate is such a waste of emotion—and a total waste of time. What good would be served if I hated the father of my great-grandson?'

But if Sophie took hate out of the equation, then what did that leave her with? An overpowering attraction which she prayed had weakened with the passing of time.

All she wanted was to have grown immune to his powerful presence and his dark, unforgettable face. After all, she hadn't seen him since just after Teodoro's baptism, a year ago, when they had brought the baby over to England.

Sophie had deliberately kept her distance from

Luis, although she'd been able to feel those steely dark eyes watching her as she moved around the room. She'd wondered if he had broken his wedding vows yet, and when she'd had a moment had asked her cousin if anything was wrong, but Miranda had just shrugged her bare brown shoulders.

'Oh, Luis should have married a docile little Spanish girl who didn't want to set foot outside the door,' she had said bitterly. 'It seems that he can't cope with a wife who doesn't whoop for joy because she happens to live in the back of beyond.'

And Sophie had directed a look of icy-blue fire across the room at Luis, meeting nothing but cold mockery in return.

Sophie's plane touched down in Pamplona in the still blazing heat of an early Spanish evening and she hurried through Customs, her eyes scanning the arrivals bay, expecting to see a driver holding a card aloft with her name on it, but it took all of two seconds to see the tall and distinctive figure waiting there.

And one second to note the hard and glittering black eyes, the unsmiling mouth and the shuttered features. He was taller than every other man there, and his face still drew the eyes of women like a magnet. No, he hadn't changed, and Sophie's heart gave a violent and unwelcome lurch.

He stood in the crowd and yet he stood alone.

It seemed that Don Luis de la Camara had come to collect her in person.

CHAPTER TWO

LUIS watched as Sophie walked through the arrivals lounge, unsmilingly observing the heads which turned to follow her as she walked, though she herself seemed completely oblivious of it. But of course she had the fair skin and hair which made the hearts of most male Spaniards melt, though none of the deliberately provocative style of her cousin.

He felt his pulse quicken and his blood thicken as she made her way towards him, her light cotton dress defining her slender legs and such delicate ankles that he was surprised they could support her weight at all. He remembered the very first time he had seen her, when she had captured his imagination with her natural beauty and grace, and such completely unselfconscious sexuality.

He had met her and wanted her in an instant and had despised the hot, sharp hunger she had inspired in him, a hunger which would never—could never—be satisfied.

And then she was standing in front of him, all honey-coloured hair and pale, translucent skin. As slender and as supple as a willow—with a look of almost grim determination glittering from the china-blue eyes.

Luis sensed danger in that determination, but he did not acknowledge it. Keeping his face a mask of formal courtesy, he inclined his head in greeting. To any other woman he might have given the traditional kiss on either cheek, but not this one. He had wanted to kiss her the first time he had seen her, but by then it was too late.

And now it was later still.

'Sophie.' A small, formal bow of his dark head. 'I trust that you have had a pleasant flight?'

He was so tall that she had to look up at him, and Sophie's heart sank as she realised that all that raw and vibrant masculinity was as intact and as potent as it had ever been. But the way he was speaking, he might as well have been enquiring about the weather. He certainly didn't sound like a bereft and newly-widowed man, and for the first time she wondered if tragedy had not, in fact, proved a convenient ending to an unhappy marriage.

She kept her face neutral—though God only knew how. 'It was smooth enough, thank-you.' Though in truth the hours had passed in a blur as she had tried to equip herself with the emotional strength to stay polite and impassive towards him.

She wondered what *his* emotional state was. Untouched, she would guess. There was no tell-tale red-rimming of the eyes, no hint that tears had been shed for the mother of his child—but then, whoever could imagine a man like Luis shedding tears?

Today, he looked remote and untouchable. His face was as cold and as hard as if it had been hewn from some pure, honey-coloured marble—but only a blind fool would have denied that he was an outrageously attractive man.

He stood at well over six feet and his shoulders were broad and strong. Lightweight summer trousers did little to conceal the powerful shaft of his thighs, and beneath the short-sleeved cotton shirt his arms looked as though they were capable of splitting open the trunk of a tree without effort.

But it was the face which was truly remarkable—it effortlessly bore the stamp of generations of Spanish aristocracy. Proud, almost cruel—with only the lush lines of his mouth breaking up the unremitting hardness of his features. A mouth so lush that it exuded the unmistakable sensuality which surrounded him like an invisible cloak.

No wonder her cousin had fallen for his devastating brand of charisma, Sophie thought, and a sudden sense of sadness left her feeling almost winded.

He saw the hint of tears which misted the Mediterranean-blue of her eyes. All the fire and determination had been wiped out, her sadness betrayed by the slight, vulnerable tremble of her lips, and he reached out to take her hand. It felt so tiny and cool when enclosed in his.

'You have my condolences, little one,' he said gravely.

She lifted her chin, swallowing the tears away, and removed her hand from his warm grasp, despairing of the not-so-subtle chemistry between them which made her want to leave it exactly where it was. 'Thank you,' she returned softly, letting her gaze fall to the ground, just in case those perceptive black eyes had the power to read exactly what was going on in her mind.

He looked at her downcast head and the stiff, defensive set of her shoulders. She was grieving for her cousin, he reminded himself—although the defiant, almost angry spark in her eyes on greeting him had little to do with grief, surely?

'Come, Sophie,' he said. 'The car awaits us and we have some drive ahead of us. Here, let me carry your suitcase for you.'

It sounded more like a command than an offer to help, and, although Sophie could have and would have carried it perfectly well on her own, she knew that it was pointless trying to refuse a man like Luis.

He would insist. Instinct told her that just as accurately as anything her cousin had ever divulged. He came from a long line of imperious men, men who saw clearly delineated lines between the roles of the sexes.

Spain might now be as modern as the rest of Europe, but men like Luis did not change with the times. They still saw themselves as conquerors—superior and supreme—and master of all they surveyed.

She could see women looking at him as they passed. Coy little side-glances and sometimes an eager and undisguised kind of hunger. She couldn't see into his eyes from here, and wondered if he was giving them hungry little glances back.

Probably. Hadn't he done just that with her, before he had discovered her identity?

And of course now, without a wife, he could behave exactly as he pleased—he could exert that powerful sexuality and get any woman he wanted into his bed.

The airport buildings were refreshingly air-conditioned, but once outside the force of the heat hit her like a velvet fist, even though the intensity of the midday sun had long since passed.

He saw her flinch beneath the impact of the raw heat, and he knew that he must not forget to warn her about the dangers of the sun. 'Why don't you take your jacket off?' he suggested suavely.

'I'll be fine,' she said tightly.

His mouth hardened. 'As you wish.'

Thankfully, the car was as cool and air-conditioned as the airport terminal, and she waited until he had driven out of the car park and was setting off towards the open road before turning to him.

'Where's Teodoro?'

'At home.'

'Oh.'

He heard the disappointment in her voice. 'You imagined that I would have brought him out on a hot summer's night to await a plane which could have been delayed?'

'So who's looking after him?'

Did her question hint at reprimand? he wondered incredulously. Did she imagine that he had left the child alone? 'He is in the charge of his *ninera*…' He saw her frown with confusion and realised that she, like her cousin, spoke almost no Spanish at all. 'His mother's help,' he translated immediately.

'Not any more,' said Sophie quietly.

'No,' he agreed heavily. There was a short, painful pause and he shot her a side-glance. 'How did your grandmother take it?'

Sophie bit her lip. Would it sound unfeeling and uncaring if she told him that, although the news had saddened her grandmother, it had come as no great surprise. What had she said? Miranda had flown far too close to the sun… But if she told Luis that then surely it would do a disservice to her cousin's memory.

'What happened, Luis? How did Miranda die?'

He pulled in a breath, choosing his words carefully, remembering that he must respect both her position and her grief.

How much of the truth did she want? he wondered. Or need?

'No one knows exactly what happened,' he said.

She knew evasion when she heard it. And faint distaste, too. She wondered what had caused it.

'There's something you're not telling me.'

He didn't answer, just kept his dark eyes straight on the road ahead, so that all she could see was his hard, shadowed profile, and Sophie said the first thing which came into her head. 'Had the driver been drinking?'

There was a short, bald silence. But what would be the point in keeping it from her? It would soon be a matter of public record.

'Sì. El habia estrado bebiendo.' He was thinking in his native language and the words just slipped out of their own accord.

She spoke hardly any Spanish, but Sophie could tell what his answer was from the flat, heavy tone of his voice. She closed her eyes in despair. 'Oh, God! Drinking very much? Do you know?'

'The tests have not yet been completed.'

A sense of outrage and of anger burned deep within her—and for the first time it was directed at Miranda instead of the man beside her. Her cousin had been a mother, for heaven's sake, with all the responsibility which went with that. She'd had a young child to look after—so how could she have been so stupid to have gone off in a car where the driver had been drinking?

Unless she hadn't known.

But Miranda hadn't been *stupid*. She'd been head-strong and impetuous sometimes, but she definitely hadn't been stupid.

Unless this man beside her, who drove the car so expertly through the darkened Spanish countryside— unless *he* had made her life such a misery that she hadn't *cared* about common sense and personal safety.

She shook her head. There was absolutely no jus-tification for Miranda going off with a drink-driver. Whatever the state of her marriage, she had always been free to walk away from it.

She shot a side-glance at the darkly angled profile. Or had she? What if Miranda had tried to walk away, taking Teodoro with her? Couldn't and wouldn't Luis have used his power and his influence to try to stop her?

She turned her head and pressed her cheek against the coolness of the window and looked out, only half taking in the wild beauty of the silhouetted landscape beyond.

The air was violet-dark and huge stars spotted the sky with splodges of silver. They looked so much bigger and brighter than the stars back in England, and her home seemed suddenly a long way away. And then she remembered. She had responsibilities, too.

Through sheer effort of will she reached down in her briefcase to retrieve her mobile phone.

'Will this work out here?' she questioned.

His eyes narrowed as they briefly glanced over at

the little technological toy. 'That depends on what type it is.' He shrugged. 'But I have another you can use, if yours can't get a signal.'

'You have a mobile phone? Here? In the car?'

His mouth twisted into a grim smile. 'Did you imagine that I communicate by bush telegraph? You will find every modern comfort, even here in La Rioja, Sophie.'

And yet his words seemed to mock the reality of his presence. 'Modern comfort,' he had said, when with his dark and brooding looks he seemed to represent the very opposite of all that was modern.

He watched as she punched out a string of numbers. 'Is your call so very important that it cannot wait until we reach the hacienda?' he questioned softly.

'I have to let someone know that I arrived safely.'

'A man, I suppose?'

'Actually, yes. It is a man.' Not that it was any of his business, but let him draw his own conclusions, which he very probably would. And obviously if it was a man then she *must* be sleeping with him!

The connection was made. 'Liam? Hi, it's me!'

Beside her, Luis stared into the abyss of the road ahead, wondering if she shared the same sexual freedom as her cousin. His gaze wandered unseen to her legs, and he was unprepared for the sudden buck of jealousy at the thought of those slender, pale limbs wrapped around the body of another.

He reminded himself that he knew women like these—with their blonde hair and their big blue eyes and their gym-toned bodies. The bodies of women but with the minds of men. They acted as men had been acting for years...they saw something they wanted and they went all out to get it.

And she had wanted him once, before she had discovered that he was to marry her cousin, just as he had wanted her—a wanting like no other. A thunderbolt which had struck him and left him aching and dazed in its wake. And it had taken her as well, he had seen that for himself, as unmistakable as the long shadows cast by the sun.

He listened in unashamedly to her conversation as the car ate up the lonely miles.

'No, I'm in the car now. With Luis.' A pause. 'Not really, no.' Another pause and then she glanced at her watch. 'It's just gone nine. No, that's OK. Yeah, I know, but I can't really talk now. Yes. OK. Thanks, Liam. I hope so, too. OK, I'll do that. I'll call you on Saturday.'

She cut the connection and put the phone back in the glove box.

'Thank you,' she said stiffly.

There was a soft, dangerous pause as he saw her cross one slim, pale leg over the other. 'Does he hunger for you already, Sophie?' he asked silkily, and the blood began to pound in his head.

She couldn't believe her ears. It was such an outrageous thing to say that for a moment Sophie was left speechless.

'I *beg* your pardon?'

He gave a half-smile in the darkness. So beautiful and so unintentionally sensual, and yet she could turn her voice to frost when it suited her.

'Actually,' she said, 'Liam is my business partner.'

'Ah.'

Something dark and sensual conveyed danger in that simple word, and Sophie felt her heart race with something more than fear. 'Is—is there going to be anyone else staying at the hacienda?'

He heard the tremor in her voice and it amused him, even while it frustrated and tempted him. Was it him she wasn't sure she trusted? Or herself? Did she want him still?

'You mean apart from Teodoro?' he questioned casually.

'You know I do.'

'One of the women from the village comes in to help with meals. And Pirro, who is my cook and gardener, lives in the hacienda with Salvadora, his wife. She is Teodoro's *ninera*—as she was mine before, when I was a child.'

'Since...when?' asked Sophie, thinking that Salvadora must be getting on a bit if she used to look after Luis. 'Since before Miranda died?'

'Oh, long before that,' he murmured evasively. 'My son is devoted to her. You will see that for yourself.'

A wave of indignation washed over her, and something far more primitive followed on its heels. Had Miranda effectively been elbowed out of the way? she wondered. The Englishwoman pushed aside for the mummy-substitute—a fellow Spaniard who could teach Teodoro the language and traditions of his father?

Well, not for much longer, vowed Sophie. Somehow she would teach him something of his mother's heritage. She scrabbled around again in her handbag, this time for a hairbrush.

His mouth curved. 'There is no one here to impress with your beauty, *mia querida*,' he drawled. Apart from him. Because when she lifted her head like that he could see the long, pure line of her neck and the perfect curve of her breasts.

'That was not my intention.' She carefully brushed out the fine, honey-coloured hair, which felt all sticky through the many hours of travelling. 'I merely wanted to make myself presentable on my arrival.' She could see distant lights. 'Are we almost there?'

'Yes, we are just about to pass through the vine-yards.'

She looked out of the window again. The famous La Camara vineyards. The largest and most impressive in the region, with grapes yielding a rich harvest which was turned into exquisite wines exported the world over.

She had once drunk La Camara Rioja herself, at a very smart dinner party in London where the host had brought the fine wine out with a reverent air and everyone had sipped it with avid and awed appreciation.

All except for Sophie. She had managed no more than a couple of mouthfuls, feeling that the stuff might choke her as she remembered the proud, arrogant face and the mocking black eyes.

'You aren't drinking, Sophie?' the host had commented.

It would have been a real party-stopper if she had explained that she was related by marriage to the owner of the vineyard, a man who made her blood sing and her temper flare in equal measure whenever she thought about him.

And she didn't want to think about him.

Muffling a little gulp, she sat back in the seat and closed her eyes.

Luis glanced over at her, frowning a little as he saw the tension which tightened her shoulders, wondering if she was about to cry, and instinctively his voice gentled. 'Did you eat on the plane?'

'No. It was horrible little bits of unrecognisable food in plastic trays. And I wasn't hungry.'

'We will have dinner when we arrive.'

'Surely it's too late for dinner?'

'But we eat very late in Spain, Sophie, did you not know that? Did you not know that the Spanish are more awake than anyone in Europe—and not only because they regard going to bed before three a.m. as a kind of personal dishonour?'

She shook her head. 'I've only ever been to Spain once, and that was for the weekend when Teodoro was baptised.'

'Then you have missed very much.' His voice had deepened now, was made almost kind with something which sounded like compassion. 'I wish this time it could be under happier circumstances, *querida*. It is a pity that you will see little of my country before you return home.'

There was an expectant silence and Sophie ignored it.

But Luis did not. 'By the way, you didn't tell me how long you were going to be staying?'

'No. No, I didn't.'

'And?'

She was glad of the darkness because the way he

framed that single syllable was nothing short of intimidating.

'I'm not sure.' Until she had reached a position of trust which ensured that she would be able to fly Teo back to England for a short holiday to see his great-grandmother. But now was definitely not the time to tell him *that*.

And then she reminded herself that as his guest he was owed certain courtesies. 'That is, I would like to stay for at least a few days, maybe longer, if that's OK with you. I'd like to see a bit of Teo.'

Unseen, his eyes narrowed. No, it was not 'OK with him.' He did not want this woman in his home for a minute longer than necessary—for reasons which were both simple and highly complex. He wanted her, but he could never have her. Not now. Not ever.

'Spaniards are famous for their hospitality, Sophie,' he said softly. 'And therefore my home is yours for as long as you wish it.'

Sophie nodded. Unless he made it impossible for her to remain, of course. 'Thank you,' she said stiffly.

'*De nada,*' he answered.

The car swept up a gravelled drive, and through the broad canopy of strange trees Sophie saw the welcoming lights of the large hacienda.

He opened the door of the car and she thought that she caught the drift of oranges and lemons, the soft night air thick with the scent of exotic blooms. She gazed at the imposing building which looked as if it had been there for ever. There was a sense of beauty, and of history, which she found impossible to ignore, despite the heartbreaking circumstances which had brought her here.

And then she was caught in the ebony glitter of those beautiful, mocking eyes.

'Welcome to my home, Sophie,' he said softly.

CHAPTER THREE

THE interior of the hacienda was cool and spacious, and their arrival must have been heard, because as soon as Luis had taken Sophie's jacket and put her suitcase down an elderly woman appeared from further down the hall. Her face creased into a warm smile as she looked up at Luis.

'*Buenas noches, Don Luis.*'

Sophie saw his hard face briefly soften with affection as he bent to kiss the woman on both cheeks.

'*Buenas noches, Salvadora.*' He said something rapidly in Spanish, and then, reverting to slow and careful English, he spoke again. 'Sophie, this is Salvadora, Teodoro's *ninera.* Salvadora, this is Sophie Mills, Miranda's cousin.'

'*Buenas noches,*' said Sophie politely, though her doubtful thoughts in the car were borne out by the woman's appearance. She really looked far too frail to be in charge of a boy aged just over a year.

Salvadora's expression was wary, Sophie thought. Her old eyes narrowed as she looked her up and down, but the wariness was replaced with a slight, formal bow.

'*Buenas noches, Señorita Mills,*' she replied slowly. 'I regret very much the sudden death of your cousin.'

Sophie bit her lip. No tears, she told herself. They could wait for later. 'Thank you.' And then, with an almighty effort, she gave a trembling smile. 'You speak very good English, Salvadora.'

Salvadora nodded in solemn acknowledgement. 'Thank you. It was always so. Don Luis had an English tutor when he was a very little boy, and so I learnt the language, too!'

Sophie tried to imagine Luis as a little boy, learning English, but it wasn't easy to picture him with the same soft, innocent face as his son.

'And, of course, it is essential that any *ninera* of Teodoro understands the language of his mother,' said a deep voice, butting into her thoughts, and Sophie turned to Luis, a question in her eyes.

'Why?'

'Because otherwise the two women would have been unable to communicate, wouldn't they?' he offered drily, seeing the look of genuine surprise on her face, and his mouth hardened. Did she imagine that he would wish to deny his son his English heritage? Did she think him some kind of devil, then?

Not for the first time, Sophie wondered why Miranda had bothered having anyone to help her with Teo at all. She hadn't had a job outside the home, nor had much to do inside the home, judging from her phone calls. She remembered how delighted her cousin had been on discovering the true extent of Luis's wealth and influence.

'He's not just gorgeous—he's *loaded,* Sophie! Absolutely loaded!'

Sophie had frowned, wondering if the financial insecurities of her childhood were blinding Miranda to reality. 'Yes, but money isn't everything. Honestly it isn't. As long as you're happy, Miranda—that's the most important thing.'

'Oh, I'm happy, all right!' Miranda had said. 'Who wouldn't be in my situation, with a man like Luis? And it's so *wonderful* having servants, Sophie, I can't tell you!'

Sophie hadn't approved of Miranda's attitude and approved of her own fleeting pang of jealousy even less. But she had said nothing. And even if she had, it wouldn't have made any difference. Miranda had always been determined to fight tooth and nail for what she wanted, and she had wanted Luis.

And who in their right mind could blame her for that?

His deep voice broke into her thoughts.

'Salvadora will show you to your room now, Sophie,' said Luis, who was watching her very closely and wondering what had caused her to frown like that, caused the tiny goosebumps that made her slender arms look so cold and so vulnerable.

That piercing black look distracted her, but she forced herself to remember the main reason why she was here. 'Can I...can I see Teodoro first? Please?'

He thought how pale she looked, and how tense— the faint shadows beneath her eyes making her lovely face look almost haunted. He shook his head decisively. 'First you should eat something.'

'But—'

'No buts, Sophie. You may shower and change first, should you wish, and then we will eat dinner.'

She wasn't used to such dominance, or to letting a man call the shots like that, and she was just about to protest when some warning light which glittered

so imperiously from the jet-dark eyes told her that her
protests would land on deaf ears. She would see her
nephew when *he* chose to let her!

And a whole meal to get through first. 'You don't
have to bother with dinner,' she said, unwilling to sit
down alone with him. Suspecting that she would find
it impossible to keep up pleasantries for an entire
meal. Or to keep forbidden thoughts at bay. 'I could
always have a sandwich in my room.'

Luis's eyes narrowed with irritation at her clumsy
refusal of his hospitality. 'It is inconceivable that a
guest should travel all this way and not be offered
sustenance. And besides, you have a long and difficult
day ahead of you tomorrow. You will join me in the
dining room.'

There he went again—commanding her instead of
asking her! What would he do if she insisted on staying in her room? Though wouldn't that be stupid? She
could hardly hide away the whole time she was here.
Better get used to eating with him, no matter how
much the idea managed to appall and yet excite her
at the same time. And surely it was inappropriate to
even be *thinking* such thoughts at a time like this?

She nodded. 'Very well. I'll get changed and come
down again.'

'I will be waiting.'

Sophie felt very slightly out of control as she followed the old woman upstairs, wondering how on
earth you could get used to having your every wish
catered for.

Although she earned a more than comfortable salary, she had always prided herself on her independence. Unlike most of her friends, she did not have

anyone to clean her apartment for her, and she did not send her shirts out to be laundered. Her mother had always drummed into her that delegating life's unpleasant tasks made you remote from life itself.

How different life appeared to be here, with gardeners and cooks and women who cared for your children.

Her shuttered room was cool and dominated by a large, plain bed, covered with snowy white linen. A vase of white flowers which she didn't recognise had been placed on the dresser and a huge fan spun around from the ceiling to shift the warm and heavy air. She would have liked to just lie down and close her eyes, but she knew that her implacable host would be waiting.

'The bathroom is through there,' pointed Salvadora. 'Is there anything you need, *señorita?*'

Peace would be close to the top of her list. But there would be no peace for Sophie, not in the foreseeable future—not with Luis present, looking like some dark and alluring angel. But she put him out of her mind because there was something far more important she needed to know.

'How is Teodoro?' she questioned falteringly, and just the mention of his name brought a little warmth creeping back into her heart. 'Is he missing his mother very much?'

Salvadora did not answer for a moment, as if she did not understand, yet it was a simple enough question.

'Of course,' said Salvadora carefully. 'He knows that something is wrong. He cries. But soon we will make him laugh again.'

Sophie felt sick. *He knows something is wrong.* Something *wrong?* The child had lost his mother, for heaven's sake, and here was Salvadora making it sound as though he had thrown his rattle out of his pram! But Salvadora had power, too. Power over Teodoro, which came from being close to him. She needed to make the older woman realise that she cared about her nephew, and that was why she was here.

'I hope to help make him laugh, too,' she said softly. 'Thank you, Salvadora. Please tell Luis that I shall be down shortly.'

'Sì, señorita.'

Sophie carefully hung up her clothes, and it was a relief to strip off her travel-crushed things and to stand beneath the invigorating jets of the shower and wash away the grit of the journey.

She plaited her still damp hair and put on a fresh cotton dress. Drawstring trousers would have made her feel more relaxed, but she suspected that an evening meal in the de la Camara house would have a certain formality to it.

She was right.

When she entered the dining room it was to see Luis already seated at a long, polished dining table laid for two and that he, too, had changed—and there was absolutely nothing she could do about the sudden rapid beating of her heart.

Gone were the short-sleeved shirt and the light-weight trousers. In their place he had donned a snowy-white shirt, a filmy garment which tantalisingly hinted at the hard, muscular torso beneath. He had left the top two buttons of the shirt unbuttoned and on view was the soft, silken gleam of olive skin, and the sprinkling of dark hair. As he rose to his feet she could see stark black trousers which hugged the narrow jut of his hips and moulded themselves to the powerful shaft of his thighs. The overall effect was to make him look like someone who had just stepped out of one of the portraits of his ancestors which lined the walls, and Sophie's mouth dried into dust.

'Good evening,' he said formally as he stood up. 'I trust that you found everything to your satisfaction?'

For a moment the power to walk properly left her and she stood unsteadily in the doorway, her trembling fingers gripping the door handle for support as she realised that she was alone with this magnificent man she both desired and feared, and in such a magnificent setting.

He knitted his dark brows together, seeing the way that her face had paled to the colour of the whitest lily, making her skin look almost translucent in comparison. Afraid that she might suddenly faint, he swiftly moved towards her.

'Something is wrong?'

Something was wrong! Everything was wrong! She was feeling everything she wasn't supposed to feel, didn't want to feel. Dark, illicit thoughts which enveloped her with tantalising fingers, locking her into forbidden fantasies. She found herself praying for some kind of merciful release. She should be concentrating on Teodoro, and on Miranda's memory—not on the bone-melting effect of her host.

She shook her head. 'No, I'm fine.'

'Then please sit down.' He pulled out a chair for

her and then returned to his own seat. 'For you do not look fine to me.'

Sophie sank down gratefully and, in an effort to distract herself, looked not into the inky glitter of his eyes but at the formality of the setting instead.

The table was set with the finest silver and fresh with flowers and gently glowing with candlelight. It was the kind of table that you would probably need a pool cue to propel the pepper and salt from one end to the other, it was so long. She could see that some cold soup had already been placed there, and never had a sandwich in her room seemed so attractive. Or so safe.

'You shouldn't have gone to all this trouble for me!' She swallowed.

'Trouble?' A dark brow was arched in arrogant query. 'I can assure you that dinner is exactly as usual.'

She supposed it was—he didn't strike her as the kind of man who would eat his dinner on a tray in front of the television! 'Oh, I see,' she said, rather weakly.

Luis studied her. He had not been expecting her down yet, imagining her to be transforming her appearance in the privacy of her room. He noticed that her face was as untouched as it had been at the airport. She had not bothered to apply any make-up and her hair was still wet from the shower. The overall effect made her look fresh and clean and much younger than her years. Almost innocent. Luis's mouth twisted into a cynical line.

He was used to women using every weapon in their armoury in order to impress him. Carefully applied make-up and gowns designed to show off magnificent cleavages, or the length of their legs. At a time like this he would not have expected finery—but he had been anticipating that a little extra effort would be made.

Clearly, Sophie Mills was not trying to impress him!

Her cotton dress was as unassuming as it was possible to be, and yet its simplicity made the curve of her high breasts all the more beguiling. She was an unnerving combination of innocence and experience, and Luis felt the slow and reluctant flicker of arousal. Perhaps the effect was deliberate, he thought. Perhaps she knew precisely how a man would react to such an innocent woman look, with her bare, pouting lips which cried out to be kissed.

'Please,' he said coolly, 'drink your soup.'

She picked up her spoon and sipped at it, but in between sips her eyes were drawn irresistibly to her host.

How daunting he looked, and not just because he had seated himself at the far end of the table. No. There was something unapproachable in the cold magnificence and the warning light which gleamed in the unfathomable depths of his eyes.

'Señor?'

Sophie looked round as a beautiful young Spanish girl appeared at the door.

'You will have some wine, Sophie?' He gestured to a dusty bottle.

She needed *something* to help her relax. 'Please.'

He murmured in Spanish and the girl immediately

poured red wine into Sophie's crystal goblet and topped up Luis's own.

Sophie drank some. 'It's…it's lovely.'

'It is a bottle from one of our finest cases.'

'Then I am honoured,' said Sophie.

He raised his glass with a thoughtful look. 'I think we must drink a toast to thank God for the life of Miranda.'

It was too much! Sophie put her glass down with a shaking hand, wondering just how hypocritical a man could be. Didn't he have any idea that Miranda might have confided in her and told her that the devastatingly handsome Don had a heart which had been chiselled from ice?

'Her life in general?' she demanded. 'Or her life here? And if that is the case then it will hardly be a joyous toast, will it, Luis?'

How passionate she sounded, he thought as the anger sizzled off her like electricity, her eyes flashing hot blue fire at him, and he met the challenge there, feeling a pulse begin to flicker into life at his temple.

'Was it such a terrible life, then?' he asked seriously.

Her gaze didn't waver, the words coming out before she had time to consider the wisdom of saying them. 'I wish to God she'd never met you,' she said bitterly.

Luis nodded slowly. But if he had never met Miranda then there would never have been a Teo—and he could not imagine a life without Teo.

How much had Miranda told her cousin? he wondered as he put his glass down on the crisp linen tablecloth and stared at her reflectively.

'Do you know how my relationship with your cousin began, Sophie?' he asked slowly.

'I know that you picked her up when she was flying!'

He stilled. 'Picked her up?' Fierce pride clipped his words out like bullets. 'You think that I am the kind of man who goes around the world propositioning air stewardesses?'

'How should I know? You've never had any shortage of women, have you? Not from what I hear!'

She made him sound like some kind of indiscriminate alley cat! 'I am not promiscuous!' he ground out. 'And I never have been!'

She gave him a cool, disbelieving look. 'Really?'

'Sophie…' he began dangerously, but then drew himself up short. She was here for probably no longer than a few days—why taint her memories and risk making the pain of loss even greater?

'What?' she questioned as she saw the shutters come down again.

He shook his head. 'Nothing.'

What was he hiding from her? What couldn't he face telling her? 'I want to hear your version of how you met,' she said stubbornly.

There was a moment of silence. 'I was flying to New York on business,' he remembered softly, and gave a wry smile. 'Your cousin served me a drink and wrote the name of her hotel on the accompanying napkin, suggesting that we meet there for a drink.'

'Which was an offer you couldn't refuse, I suppose?'

'Why should I refuse?' he asked seriously. 'She was a beautiful and vivacious girl.'

Sophie took another shaky sip of wine. 'Any woman would do, is that what you mean, just as long as she was willing?'

He felt the implacable beat of anger. And of pride. 'If that were the case,' he shrugged, 'then I would spend my whole life in bed.'

Her heart beat faster, and she was shaken by how disturbing she found his statement. 'That's a very arrogant boast, Luis.'

'It is not a boast, it is simply the truth, *querida*.' But he saw the paleness of her face and relented. She was tired, and overwrought and full of sorrow. 'Come,' he said quietly. 'Let us drink our soup in peace, and talk no more on this subject.'

Sophie shook her head. She wanted to make some sense of her cousin's life here—which at the moment seemed like an out-of-focus picture. Miranda's contact with her had been erratic—and usually when she was in the midst of one of the many crises which had seemed to dog her all her life.

'I want to know. I want to hear your side of it.'

She spoke as if he were standing on trial, he thought bitterly. For the sake of his son and the de la Camara name, he would not be judged and found wanting! 'Very well,' he continued. 'I will not deny that I was flattered by her attentions. When a very beautiful woman makes no attempt to disguise her desire for you, what man wouldn't be?'

'But you intended it to be a one-night stand, I suppose?'

He stared at her uncomprehendingly. 'A *one-night stand?*' he repeated incredulously. 'What joy and pleasure and fulfilment can be gained from such a liaison as that?'

She heard the raw vitality in his voice and saw the passion which animated the proud, handsome face. And for one brief moment Sophie realised that by chasing Luis Miranda had flown *very* close to the sun. And had paid the price. To have known such a man intimately, and to have borne his child, must indeed have taken her to dizzy heights from which there could only be a plummeting descent.

For with an inexplicable but blinding certainty Sophie recognised the elusiveness which lay at the very core of Don Luis's character. A man who would only ever give a part of himself to a woman. His body, yes. But his heart? She wondered if a man like this actually had a heart. Or if, as Miranda had once claimed, it was made of ice and not of beating flesh and blood.

'So you were offering her a future, is that it?'

He shrugged as he took some bread and broke it. 'Relationships do not have two extremes,' he pointed out coolly. 'There is something midway between a one-night stand and marriage.'

'You mean an affair?'

'An affair implies that one of the partners is married to someone else, which was not true in our case.' He paused. 'I would have called it a relationship.'

'What a grown-up and yet cold-hearted word you make that sound.'

'I did not mean to. And it was a very enjoyable relationship—for a time, at least.'

'But a baby changed it, I suppose?'

There was a short, tense silence. 'Yes, Sophie,' he

said eventually, his voice expressionless. 'A baby changes everything.'

'And...and...if she hadn't been pregnant, would you have married her?'

He met her gaze unfalteringly, wondering just how he had been coerced into talking so frankly to a woman in this way. And recognising that much more of telling the truth would hurt her. And for what purpose?

'I think this conversation has gone on long enough, don't you, Sophie?' he said gently.

'Tell me,' she pleaded.

'I think you know the answer to your question, deep down, don't you?'

'So you didn't love her?' she breathed. 'You married her, but you didn't love her!'

'You ask impossible questions!'

'Not impossible,' she argued. 'Difficult, maybe— but not impossible.'

There was a long, fraught silence before he spoke. 'I do not think that I know what love is!' he said quietly. 'Do you? All I know is that Miranda was pregnant, and that it was my duty to marry her. And my responsibility.'

Duty.

Responsibility.

These were not the words of a man who had loved and lost, and with an aching heart Sophie accepted that the proud Spanish aristocrat had never really loved her cousin.

'And did she know that it was duty? Did you drive that message home to her, that she was only your wife

because of circumstance? Is that why she was so unhappy?'

'The subject is closed!' he snapped. 'I will not discuss it further. Now eat your soup, Sophie.'

She opened her mouth to object, but the black eyes
glittered tellingly and Sophie realised that she had
said enough. More than enough. Why make him angry? A disconcerting enough thought in itself—but
the fall-out from that anger would be self-defeating.
She needed to have access to her nephew, and for that
she needed Luis on her side...

'Eat!' he said once more, and then unexpectedly
his voice softened. 'Please.'

With the brittleness gone from his voice, some of
the fight went out of her, and she ate, hungrier than
she had imagined. The gazpacho was delicious. As
was the omelette studded with sweet herbs which followed and then a creamy little wedge of flan. Sophie
ate every bit, and when she had finished she looked
up to find him wryly studying her.

'You were very hungry,' he observed gravely.

'Yes.' She tried to remember the last time she had
eaten a complete meal. Not since his telephone call,
and that was two days ago. 'Well, I haven't had much
appetite lately.'

'No. Of course you haven't.' He put his napkin
down on the table. 'Come, Sophie. You should sleep
now.'

She shook her head. 'Not yet.' She rose unsteadily
to her feet and met the question in his eyes. 'Please,
Luis,' she forced herself to say, recognising that in
this, at least, he had total control, 'I would like to see
Teodoro now.'

He would rather she wait until the morning. She looked too pale and too fragile at this time of night— as if when she stepped forward she might tumble into his arms at any moment, and he had to quash the thought of how much that would please him. But he could read the determination in the stubborn lift of her chin, and he gave a small sigh. 'Very well. Come with me.'

Breathing a sigh of relief, she followed him upstairs, feeling disturbed and guilty by the fact that she couldn't tear her eyes away from each movement of his body. She shouldn't be feeling this way. Not now and not with *him*—and especially not at a time like this. Wanting him should have left her a long time ago, been replaced with a feeling of detachment. So where the hell was the detachment now?

Through a maze of corridors they passed, until he stopped outside a door and turned to her.

'Now you must be very quiet,' he warned softly. 'He has been sleeping fretfully of late, and on no account must we wake him.'

'Is it any wonder he's been sleeping fretfully?' she whispered back. 'Babies are instinctive—he must be missing his mother like mad.'

He seemed about to say something, but then appeared to change his mind, putting one finger over his lips. 'Shhh! No more. Come,' he murmured.

They moved silently into the room like two people doing an impersonation of Santa Claus, and once they were by the large, old-fashioned wooden crib Sophie's heart flipped a somersault.

She had not seen Teodoro since his baptism, when he'd been a few weeks old. A few infrequent photos from Miranda had come her way, the most recent taken on his first birthday.

But nothing could have prepared her for the emotional impact of seeing Miranda's sleeping child lying there, oblivious to the world.

His rosy mouth was puckered and two angelic arcs of thick, dark lashes curved above the apple-plumpness of his cheeks. The curls of his hair looked jet-dark against the pillow and Sophie thought that she could see the faint trace of dried tears on his face.

So innocent and helpless, she thought, tears misting her eyes. And he would wake in the morning and be miserable for his mother and unable to articulate why. Poor, darling Teo!

Instinctively she reached her hand out to smooth away a lock of hair, but in an instant it was caught in an iron-fast grip before she could reach it.

'No,' he breathed, in a voice soft with threat.

And before Sophie could stop him he had hauled her unceremoniously out of the room and quietly shut the door behind them.

He still had her by the wrist and she could feel his strong fingers biting into her flesh, just as she could almost feel the palpable rage which lit angry fire behind the black eyes. He was too close to ignore. Too close for comfort and yet not close enough.

Every pore in her body seemed to scream out that he was within touching distance, and for one mad and delirious moment Sophie wanted to touch him above all else, just as she had done the very first time she laid eyes on him. To lose herself in the cradle of those strong arms, to rest her weary head on those broad shoulders, to feel the hard, lean power of his body.

'I told you not to waken him, *señorita,*' he ground out furiously. 'Did you want that we should have an inconsolable child crying for the rest of the night?'

'I…I wasn't thinking,' she protested, snatching her wrist away from his hand, feeling the frenzied flutter of her pulse beneath his strong, hard fingers and wondering if he had felt it, too. And wondering if he would guess that it was inspired by desire, and not by fear or anger.

'No,' he said grimly, and her trembling mouth and darkened eyes wakened a sudden pulse of need in him which only added to his fury. 'You didn't think. Well, try thinking now, *querida*. Teodoro is a child and not a toy—you don't just pick him up on a whim in the middle of the night, no matter what the circumstances, and especially not in *these* circumstances. Try thinking of him and of *his* needs, and not your own!' he finished bitterly.

Sophie stared at him. She had tried her best to keep her dislike of him hidden, but it seemed that he had no qualms about doing likewise.

She took a sure and protective step back. 'Goodnight, Luis,' she said coldly. 'I'm going to bed now.'

CHAPTER FOUR

LUIS stared down at the bent blonde head, thinking how ridiculously young she looked wearing black. 'Sophie?'

Sophie looked up at him blankly. 'What?'

He handed her a tiny cup containing coffee as ebony-black as his eyes. 'Here. Take this. Drink it!' he ordered softly.

In a daze, she nodded and took it from him. But then, she had spent most of the day feeling as though she was on autopilot, following the flower-decked coffin like a disbelieving robot. 'Thank you.'

He watched her sip it through frozen lips. She looked tiny—almost doll-like—as she hunched up in one of the oversized chairs he had gently sat her down on. Against the whiteness of her skin, her blue eyes dominated her face like saucers, the lashes feathering out like stars.

He gave a low sigh as some of the tension left him, relieved that the day would soon be over. The funeral had been both ornate and sombre, with four priests performing it out of respect for Luis's position, rather than because Miranda had been particularly religious.

'Are you feeling a little better now?' he asked softly.

'Yes.' Sophie was just glad that it was all over, another page turned, another ordeal behind her. Somehow she had survived the day. There had been a late arrival of a group of lavishly dressed, bright-eyed twenty-and thirty-somethings, who, Luis had informed her, rather grimly, were Miranda's own little clique. But mostly the church had been filled with friends and family of Luis—his mother and father had flown from Madrid for the service, and a car had just taken them back to the airport.

Luis's mother had given her a curious stare, but she had embraced her, and Sophie had been grateful for that. She knew from Miranda that their relationship had not been a good one— 'She thinks he should have married some cute little Spanish girl,' she had once said.

But the grief of Luis's mother had seemed genuine and Sophie had falteringly accepted her condolences.

She looked around the room. Everyone had gone, and now it was just the two of them left in the elaborate and rather formal sitting room. In his dark clothes, Luis looked impossibly formal, a black-haired and black-suited stranger—a few short steps and yet a million miles away from her.

'Where is Teodoro?' she asked.

'Salvadora is bathing him.'

'Isn't it a little early for that?'

'I think that I am the better judge of my son's welfare, don't you?' he responded blandly.

Sophie bit her lip in frustration. She had barely seen the child since she had been practically hauled from his room last night by his angry father, who seemed to imagine that she had been trying to wake him up on purpose.

And today he had been brought to the church in a

separate car with Salvadora, and had clung to her neck throughout.

Sophie met Luis's look of indifference with a sudden flare of defiance. 'Luis—are you trying to keep me away from my nephew?'

He raised his dark eyebrows, as though she had just said something completely incomprehensible. 'Why should I do something like that?'

'I should have thought that it was fairly obvious! You don't want me to get to know him, do you, or, more importantly, for him to get to know me?'

'Dios!' he said, heatedly now. 'The child is feeling lost and confused—'

'Well, of course he is—he's just lost his mother!'

He opened his mouth to reply and then seemed to think better of it, and Sophie looked at him in frustration. 'Haven't you got an answer to that? Can't you even begin to try to imagine what it must be like for a little child—one moment she's there, and the next…?' Her words tailed off and she expelled a long, low breath.

She was making it very difficult for him.

She looked up, her eyes bright. 'Well?'

'Sophie, it is not quite as you imagine it to be,' he said heavily. 'It could be worse.'

'How?'

He chose his words with care, picking them out as if they had been deep thorns embedded in his flesh. 'Miranda was not the kind of mother who was with Teo every waking hour.'

She heard the hint of something unknown in his voice. 'Are you trying to tell me she was a bad mother?'

'I am saying that she wasn't…around—not for a lot of the time. She left most of Teodoro's care to Salvadora—you must have seen the evidence of that for yourself today. Anyone can see that my son is completely devoted to her.'

She didn't want to believe him, but his words had a ring of truth to them, and Sophie bit her lip as she remembered Miranda talking about life as a mother. Hadn't her cousin said herself that motherhood wasn't all it was cracked up to be? Hadn't she told Sophie that you never appreciated freedom until it was taken away from you?

Sophie frowned. Had Miranda neglected her son by her absences—and could it have been Luis's behaviour which had driven her away? Her inability to cope with his regard for other women perhaps? She studied his impassive face. Even if that *had* been the case, was there any point in letting that deter her from her real objective for being here? What good would blame and reproach do Teo?

He stared at the indignant set of her lips, and sighed. 'What do you want, Sophie? Tell me, honestly, and I will give my consideration to your desires.'

But, to her startled horror, she felt little shivers begin to skitter across her skin, his murmured words reminding her that their meaning could be interpreted in more than one way. Was it just a trick of nature which was making her warm with the slow unfurling of need? she asked herself in silent despair. Nature's ruthless way of ensuring that the living carried on in every way that mattered? Didn't death only accentuate the life force?

She swallowed, focusing on facts and not on her body's weakness. 'I'll tell you what I want, Luis,' she said slowly. 'I want time for my nephew to learn to know me and to love me—'

'To *love* you?' he repeated incredulously.

'Is that such a crime?'

'No, no crime. But do you really think that these things can happen overnight?'

'Of course I don't. But neither do they happen if I am to be continually kept at arm's length. I would have liked to see him having his bath—'

'I thought that you would be tired,' he said coolly. 'And too upset today to cope with Teodoro's domestic routine.'

'Like you are, I suppose?'

He shook his dark head. 'I make no pretence, not even to you, Sophie. I grieve for a young life uselessly wasted, but I will shed no tears on my pillow tonight.'

'Have you—have you no heart?'

The black eyes narrowed thoughtfully. 'Who knows?' he answered softly. 'Some would say not. Women have said it for most of my adult life, but I will tell you this, Sophie—where my son is concerned, I most definitely *do* have a heart, and with it a determination that nothing or no one will ever harm him. Do I make myself clear?'

Crystal-clear. There was no mistaking the threat underpinning the rich, deep voice and a different woman might very easily have been intimidated by the sheer force of personality which he so effortlessly exuded. But she had something to fight for—or, rather, someone. And the knowledge that she was fighting for Teodoro gave her the strength to return the challenge of his gaze.

'I have no intention of ever harming Teodoro, Luis.'

'And no desire to paint his father as a black-hearted demon?'

'Even if I thought that…' She met the proud hauteur in that gaze without flinching. 'Even if I did—I would not dream of trying to warp a tiny child's perception. You may be no friend of mine, Luis—but our relationship is not what is at stake here. My relationship with Teodoro *is*.'

'But you have no real relationship with Teodoro,' he stated quietly.

'No, you're right, I don't,' she admitted. 'And I might never have done—more than the occasional family celebration.' She put her empty coffee cup down. 'But things have changed,' she continued quietly. 'What went on before is irrelevant now. Miranda is dead and I want her son to have the opportunity to get to know the other side of his family. To learn something of his English roots. Starting now.'

His eyes narrowed. *'Now?'* he echoed quietly.

'Right this very moment.' She nodded, and rose slowly to her feet, smoothing down the skirt of her black linen dress. 'Once Teodoro is bathed, I would like to read him a bedtime story. I assume that you have no objections to that, Luis?'

A shaft of sunlight had filtered through the shuttered windows and illuminated her hair to spun gold. With her white, untouched skin contrasting so markedly against the black dress, she looked so pure, he thought, and a slow pulse began to flicker at his temple.

'Of course I have no objections,' he answered huskily. 'But you will not object if I am there also?'

'You think perhaps I might attempt to spirit him away without your knowledge?'

He resisted the urge to answer with the logical reply that she had no passport for his son, because the principle here was far more important than the practicality. Sophie Mills needed to be very clear where he stood and where she stood.

'Try anything like that, Sophie,' he said in a soft voice of dangerous threat, 'and you will know what it is to enrage me. I am a de la Camara, and nothing which is truly mine will ever be taken from me. Do you understand?'

The hard features had tightened with some dark, atavistic emotion, transforming him into an adversary most people wouldn't dream of taking on, and for a moment Sophie despaired. Oh, why had her cousin chosen to hitch her star to such a man? Why couldn't she have settled down and been happy with one of the countless other men who had adored her?

Because Don Luis was unobtainable—that much was apparent. And hadn't Miranda always delighted in the pursuit of something which eluded her so completely?

The black eyes glittered. 'Do you understand?'

And suddenly a wave of reactive relief washed away some of the tension. The worst of the day was over—and she was going to read her nephew a story! 'Oh, for goodness' sake—don't overreact, Luis! I'll go and get a story-book from my room.'

For the first time that day, he smiled. 'Very well. I will bring Teodoro down here to wait for you.'

In her room Sophie took the opportunity to change out of the stark black dress and slipped into a pair of old jeans and a faded green singlet which had seen better days. But babies were babies, even if they were newly bathed! She didn't want to worry if he dribbled on her clothes or was sick. She wanted to relax completely and she badly wanted to cuddle Teo.

She picked up one of several books she had brought with her, and a brightly wrapped package, and closed the bedroom door behind her.

Quietly she descended the dark and sweeping staircase and walked back along to the sitting room, but when she reached the open door she stood completely still, her startled eyes taking in the scene which lay before her.

Luis was stretched out on the carpet, playing with his son. He must have discarded his jacket and his tie, and loosened the top few buttons of his snowy shirt, for a distracting glimpse of dark olive skin was on show.

He hadn't seen her—his attention was all on the pyjama-suited chubbiness of his young son, who was squealing with laughter and shouting, 'Papa! Papa!' And Luis was laughing too, throwing his dark head back with uninhibited pleasure.

She sucked in a raw breath of disbelief, because he was now pulling funny faces and was almost unrecognisable. Was this really Luis de la Camara? she wondered dazedly.

His black eyes had softened, and so had his mouth—curved into an indulgent and affectionate smile as a fat little fist curled over the hard definition of his shoulder. He threw his head back to chuckle again as small fingers moved up to graze over the shadowed jut of his jaw, and with that rich and sonorous sound something inside Sophie sprang to unwelcome life.

She had always understood his physical appeal—that would have been apparent to just about any woman on the planet—but this Luis, this soft and tender Luis, caught her completely off guard.

She had never seen him so relaxed, nor so at ease with himself. He looked…he looked almost *boyish* as he murmured something in Spanish into Teodoro's ear.

She tried to tell herself that it was just instinct which made the pit of her stomach begin to dissolve. Just like the instinct which made you swat at a fly if it buzzed too close to your eye. And instinct wasn't rational—it was random and cruel.

She shook her head as if to deny that it was anything more than physical attraction—because that was easy enough to hold in check. Far more dangerous was to start getting all dreamy about him and attributing qualities to him which he simply did not possess. He loved his son, that was all. *That was all.*

He looked up then, and his face changed as if by magic. It was almost as if some impenetrable shutter had suddenly descended, for his features stilled and his face lost something of its vitality and animation.

And maybe Teodoro sensed the change in his father too, for he suddenly turned his dark and curly head to stare at Sophie with wide, questioning eyes.

The innocence and confusion that she read in them

made a lump catch in Sophie's throat and she walked towards him, the hand which held the book and the present trembling with the emotion of seeing him again. Part her. Part *her* flesh and blood, too, as well as Luis's.

She dropped to her knees onto the floor in front of him, her delight at seeing him again making her impervious to the fact that Luis's long legs were sprawled only inches away from her.

'Hello, Teodoro, darling,' she said softly, but she could hear the break in her voice.

Teodoro continued to stare at her, his little face solemn.

Luis spoke softly in Spanish. 'Teodoro—this is your cousin Sophie. You met her once when you were very tiny.'

'Hello, darling,' she said again, and, to her mortification, the little boy's lips began to tremble and he buried his face in his father's shoulder, but not before Sophie had seen the tears which slid from between the thick black lashes of his eyes and the little shake of his shoulders as he gave a muffled sob.

'Oh, Teodoro,' she whispered helplessly. 'Please don't cry.'

'*Ssh, mi querido hijo!*' crooned Luis. Balancing his son in the cradle of his arm, he sat up and continued to murmur to Teodoro in Spanish, in the softest and sweetest way that Sophie could ever imagine a man doing.

And *she* had made him cry!

Luis glanced up to see her stricken face, and felt an unwilling tug of empathy as he felt his son quieten in his arms.

'Do not blame yourself, *querida*,' he said quietly. 'It is a difficult time for him.'

She met his gaze and saw a look of understanding there which took her breath away. 'Yes.'

'See.' His long, olive fingers wound themselves between the ebony curls on Teodoro's head. 'He cries no more.'

Sophie nodded, wondering if the child would ever cuddle *her* the way he was cuddling his father. It didn't seem likely.

Luis picked up the book, and then said something else in Spanish to Teodoro, who nodded against his shoulder and then slowly turned around.

'Shall we read the book together?' he questioned. 'With Sophie? Come. Come, Sophie.'

He gestured to one of the long sofas. Feeling suddenly almost stricken with shyness, Sophie followed him over to it, and he waited until she had sat down before sprawling upon it himself. He stretched out his legs with a kind of careless grace, with Teodoro clinging on to him like a little monkey all the while.

She perched on the edge of the seat, catching the faint scent which was a beguiling mixture of aftershave and masculinity, and fumblingly she opened the book.

Luis leaned over to look at it, and the aftershave became even more distracting.

'What is the story?' he asked.

'It's a book of nursery rhymes,' she said tentatively.

She had thought carefully about what to bring, deliberating and agonising over her choice of book, terrified of evoking painful memories of Miranda.

'I hope you like nursery rhymes, Teodoro?'

'Canciones infantil,' interpreted Luis, and Teodoro wriggled himself forward, his attention caught by a beautiful illustration of a silver nutmeg and a golden pear.

'Do you know this one?' asked Sophie.

'He knows only Spanish stories,' said Luis.

But surely Miranda must have read to her son in English?

'Well, this is an English story with a mention of Spain, so it seems perfect! Now, listen, Teo. "I had a little nut tree and nothing would it bear..."' As she began to recite the poem, her voice taking on a slow and rhythmical resonance, Teodoro listened, seemingly enraptured. And when she got to the bit about "the King of Spain's daughter came to visit me, and all for the sake of my little nut tree!", Luis laughed, and Sophie found herself laughing with him.

The laughter broke the ice completely and melted it away as Sophie read about ten of the rhymes, until there was a light brush of her arm, and she turned to find Luis's dark eyes fixed on her, their expression rueful.

'It is late, *querida,*' he said. 'See how sleepy Teodoro grows.'

She could see the boy rubbing his fist in his eyes and stifling a yawn as he struggled to listen to more rhymes, and she closed the book. 'I could read you some more stories tomorrow, Teodoro,' she whispered. 'Would you like that?'

Just for good measure, Luis repeated the question in Spanish and she was rewarded with the briefest of nods, which sent his dark curls dancing, and then he jammed a thumb into the corner of his mouth and snuggled back into his father's shoulder.

She looked up as Luis rose to his feet and scraped a silky handful of hair back from her face. 'Can I— can I help you to put him to bed?'

Luis froze, arrested by the movement which suddenly shattered his equilibrium. The way she scooped away her hair only drew attention to the breasts which danced beneath the faded T-shirt, and his eyes narrowed as he felt the unmistakable beat of desire. He felt the heat and the unwelcome hardening of his body, and silently he cursed her, even though the provocation had been unconscious, not deliberate.

'No,' he said flatly. 'Not tonight.'

She raised her eyebrows at him in question and this time he arrogantly mouthed the word no again, over his son's head.

Sophie shot him a defiant look. She wasn't about to start making a scene in front of Teodoro, but she wasn't going to let it rest, either. How dared he blow so hot and cold with her? Acting as though she had made an outrageous request, when all she had done was ask to help put the child to bed! And this after what she thought had been a very amicable reading session.

But she gave Teodoro a gentle smile. 'Goodnight,' she said softly, and then for good measure she added, *"Buenas noches!"* and was rewarded with a quick little quirk of a mouth which told her exactly what a young Luis's lips must have looked like.

Luis expelled a hissing breath as he carried his son up the stairs, waiting for the dull ache of desire to gradually subside.

Maldecir! he thought to himself. *Damn* her.

His body was hungry—his senses on fire with a clamour which made him feel weak. What did she do to him, and how? And why had time only sharpened his hunger, not dulled it, as time so often did?

In Teodoro's room he watched and waited and stroked the dark tumble of curls until the little boy had fallen into a slow and steady sleep. Only then did he allow himself to suck in a shuddering lungful of air as he stood watching his son.

Poor, innocent *niño,* he thought, with bitter sadness. His mother buried today and all his father could think about were the insistent calls of his own physical needs.

Sophie took her place opposite him at supper that evening in a headachy mood. She said little during the first two courses and ate even less, but she drank two full glasses of La Camara Rioja, and some of the tension left her.

'The chicken is good?' Luis frowned.

'It is very good.'

'Then why don't you eat a little more of it?'

But her answer was stalled by the ringing of the telephone, and moments later Salvadora came in.

'Don Luis?'

Luis glanced up. *'Sí?'*

'It is Alejandra,' she said quickly.

Luis nodded and rose to his feet, but not before Sophie had seen the thoughtful frown in his eyes. 'Will you excuse me?'

'Of course.'

She tried to listen to his conversation, just as he

had listened to hers with Liam, but she couldn't make out a word of the quick-fire Spanish. Whoever Alejandra was, he was certainly very intimate with her, judging by the way in which he spoke.

But when he came back into the room she thought he seemed edgy, the handsome face shadowed and tense. Several times she saw him glance down at his watch.

Eventually, she put her coffee-cup down with a clatter. 'Am I keeping you from something, Luis?'

'You do look a little tired, *querida,*' he observed.

'Yes,' she agreed. 'And so do you, for that matter.'

'Might I suggest that you retire to your room at the earliest opportunity?' he said, his eyes trying not to linger on the sleek, creamy column of her neck. 'It has been a long day.'

'And you? Are you planning an early night yourself?'

Luis's mouth hardened and a pulse began to work at his temple. Did she imagine that having houseroom gave her the right to question him about his arrangements?

'I have to go out,' he said silkily. 'If you have no objections?'

She wondered what he would do if she said that yes, she had. Would he cancel whatever was making him seem so distracted? And yet, perhaps, in a way it would be better if he went out.

She could phone Liam and check her e-mails. Do all the normal things which usually occupied her mind, instead of remembering this terrible day and trying to keep her thoughts away from this black-eyed Don who had now risen to his feet.

He stood looking down at her, with fingers splayed carelessly across his narrow hips, stretching the dark material of his trousers tautly over the powerful shafts of his thighs.

And, shockingly, Sophie couldn't tear her eyes away from him, feeling her throat dry to dust and forcing herself to pay attention as her fumbling fingers folded the linen napkin. Yes, much better that he went out, as far away from her as possible.

'Of course I have no objections,' she said thickly.

He took one last look at her. She looked as beautiful as any woman he had ever seen. The candle light was transforming her hair into bright, liquid honey which fell like angels' wings on either side of her face. Did she realise that when she spoke to him she sometimes snaked the point of her pink tongue along her lips? Making them gleam more enticingly than if they were painted with the finest cosmetics.

Had she come to his home with the deliberate intention of taunting him with what he could never have? And did she not realise that her obvious dislike of him was having no effect on him at all, making absolutely no difference to the tension which always seemed to pulse in the air whenever they were together. *'Buenas noches, señorita,'* he bade her, the courteous formality made meaningless by the sudden roughening of his voice. 'I will see you in the morning. Please don't wait up.'

She looked up, and her voice was as cold as her eyes. 'Why ever would I want to wait up for you, Luis?'

CHAPTER FIVE

THE room and the house seemed curiously empty once Luis had gone. And, even though Sophie knew that Salvadora and Pirro were still around, and that Teodoro was sleeping upstairs, shadows and ghosts of the past seemed to rise up to haunt her.

She tried to imagine Miranda sitting in here, eating the beautifully prepared food in the beautiful dining room, but it was a hard stretch of the imagination. The house was exquisite, but so isolated. And Miranda had always been such a people-magnet, always preferring parties to privacy. Had she bothered to think through the reality of Luis's lifestyle before she had married him? Sophie wondered.

She drank a small cup of the deliciously strong coffee which Salvadora had left on the table and then, when her yawns could no longer be stifled, she went upstairs and took a long shower before climbing into bed.

The bed was wide and welcoming, but sleep took a long time coming, and when it did come it provided no welcome refuge, because her dreams gave her no peace. For the nature of the dreams was as disturbing as the identity of the man who inhabited each and every one with such dangerous and sensual stealth.

Luis.

Strong and lean, his dark figure mocking her from afar, the black eyes tempting her as they always had done. She reached out for him, but the air was empty, the promise of him as false as a mirage.

She grew warm, then cool, and then warm again. Distractedly she touched her skin to find it bathed with the slick of sweat. Only half-awake, she pushed the linen sheet from her body, tossing and turning, moaning a protest against the rapid thundering of her heart, unable to rid herself of the powerful image of the proud Spaniard with the cold, hard face and the hot, hard body.

His face swam in front of her, and this time—this time surely she could reach him? For one moment he caught her in his arms, crushed her to his chest, a second away from kissing her, but then he shook his head in contemptuous dismissal, pushed her back down on the bed and turned away.

A heartfelt moan of protest was torn from her lips.

'Luis!'

Luis was tiptoeing past her room when he heard a startled cry coming from the direction of Sophie's room and he stilled.

He stood silently outside the door when another sound greeted him—only this time a kind of moaned sob. And his name. She was crying out his name! *His* name! Sweet God in heaven! His gut twisted and something in the quality of her cry made him ache unbearably.

Softly he twisted the handle and pushed the door open and then stilled, becoming as motionless as stone as his eyes grew accustomed to the light.

'*Mi Dios!*' he breathed, almost imperceptibly.

She must have opened the shutters, for moonlight spilled through the window with an incandescent light

which painted her silver, like some creature from a
fable. She wore a tiny scrap of a nightgown, some
slippery pale garment which had ridden up over her
knees.

Her hair lay gleaming across the pillow, while one
arm was stretched with abandon above her head, and
as he watched she moved, one slim and delectable
thigh sending a tantalising shadow shafting across her
body, so that she was all light and dark.

Luis felt the thick, honeyed pulse of desire as he
watched her, saw her turn again, saw her frown, still
in the throes of sleep, and he wondered what had
caused that sudden look of distress.

Madre de Dios!

Was she dreaming?

Or was he?

He wondered if he should wake her, but could he
trust himself to approach her pale beauty? What if
she awoke to find him in her room, towering over her
bed, his face tight with the tension which her unconscious sensuality had unwittingly produced—then
might she not scream the house down?

Uncaring of the folly of his actions, he moved silently towards the bed, staring down at her, noting the
faint sheen of sweat which made her skin gleam as if
it was lit from within, and again he felt the aching
heat of desire.

But it was nothing other than an unendurable tor-
ture to stand and watch her, and he bit his lip, preparing to take his leave of her.

Sophie's eyes flew open and she saw the lean,
proud face, his eyes blacker than she had ever seen
them as they stared down at her, and even in the

moonlight she could see a dull flush darkening the aristocratic curve of his cheekbones.

'Luis!' she breathed in disbelief, as if her dream had suddenly taken living, breathing form.

He shuddered out the words, 'I heard you call out.' But he omitted to tell her exactly what it was that she had called. 'I thought that perhaps you were having a nightmare, *querida*.'

She sat up, oblivious to the spill of her breasts over her nightgown, aware only of their tingling, their ache, their growing tenderness as he continued to stare at her like that.

Her hand flew to her throat. 'What—what time is it?'

He swallowed. 'It is late—or, rather, it is very early. Four o'clock and the birds have not yet begun to sing. Go back to sleep, now, Sophie. Sleep. Sleep, *querida*. You need to sleep.'

She had never heard his voice so soft, nor so beguiling, and she settled back down against the pillows.

'Sleep,' he urged again, and she pulled the sheet up to her chin, for which he both damned and applauded her.

He stood there, watching the drift of her lashes as they curved down over her darkened eyes, heard her sigh—once, twice.

He waited until her breathing was steady, and then, with the aching which now seemed to have invaded every pore of his body, he moved stiffly away from the bed.

He shut the door as quietly as he had opened it and then, once he had checked on Teodoro, went to his bathroom and took a fierce, cold shower. He lay in bed, watching with empty eyes as the dawn crept in through the window.

Sophie awoke with a heavy head and a curious sense of disorientation which a long bath didn't quite banish. And, when she eventually went downstairs to where breakfast had been laid up on the sunlit and flower-filled terrace, it was to find Luis's place empty.

Half-heartedly she spread jam on sun-warmed bread and looked up at Salvadora, who was pouring coffee.

'Luis has already eaten breakfast?'

Salvadora hesitated. 'No, *señorita*. Don Luis has not yet been down.'

Had he come in late, then? Sophie stared unseeingly at her plate as fragments of a troubled dream came back to taunt her.

Salvadora deposited a dish of fresh fruit in front of her. 'You would perhaps like some eggs?'

'No.' Sophie shook her head. 'Thank you, no. Bread will be fine.'

But once Salvadora had gone Sophie ate very little, then pushed her plate away and sat looking at the beauty of her surroundings.

It really was the most idyllic place she had ever seen. The sky was unbelievably blue, and in the distance was the acid-yellow hue of the lemon trees, hung heavy and fragrant with fruit. She stood up and went to lean over the balustrade, staring ahead at the formal and beautifully laid-out gardens. It was a very peaceful place, she thought.

She thought of the solitude of the hacienda, the isolation of Miranda's position as a foreign wife, so far from home, and a great wave of sadness washed over her, knowing that her cousin had made the wrong choice in coming here.

And if Miranda had not done that—then might there not have been a chance for Sophie?

She sighed. Of course there wouldn't. It was only through Miranda that she had met him. Fate had never intended her to become involved with Luis de la Camara, and she must never forget that.

'Oh, Miranda,' she whispered helplessly as guilty tears began to slide from beneath her lashes. Would she have been shocked or surprised to know that Sophie had always secretly coveted her husband? Forgive me, prayed Sophie silently.

Luis saw her from inside the house, and knew she was crying even before he was close enough to see the faint glimmer of tears shimmering on her pale cheeks.

He flinched as if he had inflicted the tears himself, but maybe it was best that she cried, for these were the first tears that he had seen.

'Sophie?' he said softly.

She heard his footfall, but didn't turn her head, dabbing instead at her eyes with the napkin, not wanting him to see her looking so lost and so vulnerable. And dreading that those clever black eyes might guess at part of her guilty secret.

'Why are you crying?' he questioned, close enough to touch the silken gold of her hair, and he clenched his fist deep in the pocket of his trousers to stop himself.

She shook her head and swallowed down the last of them. 'Nothing. I'm—I'm OK now.'

'No,' he asserted gently. 'Tell me why you are crying.'

His softness dissolved all her defences. 'I was j-just...' her voice trembled '...thinking about Miranda. Wishing that it could have been—'

'Different?' he put in, and she nodded. 'Ah, Sophie,' he said softly. 'Sophie.'

His words drew her into his arms as surely as if they had been magnetic and she went into them, the tears streaming down her face.

'It's OK,' he soothed, and his hand went up automatically to smooth down her hair, his fingertips lingering on its silken softness. 'It's OK.'

But even in the midst of the storm his touch made her senses go into overdrive. The warmth of him. The lean hardness of him. His scent, so evocatively and so provocatively masculine. She could feel her breasts, first cushioning and then hardening against the muscular torso, and before the honey-rush of desire could overwhelm her, warning bells began to sound in her subconscious.

She had dreamed of him! 'You were in my room in the middle of the night!' she accused.

He wished she had not reminded him, for the memory began to produce an ache which was distinctly uncomfortable. 'I heard you call out,' he husked. 'I was concerned. I merely came in to check that you were OK.'

All of a sudden she felt acutely embarrassed as she remembered the dream and wondered just what she *had* called out, and it was easier and less disturbing to focus on what *he* had been doing there. 'You'd been out, hadn't you?' She frowned. 'It was very late.'

'Yes. I was on my way back to my room when I heard you.'

'And you'd been out to see a woman. The woman who called you during dinner. *Alejandra*,' she remembered.

'Alejandra,' he agreed. 'That is correct.'

Something in the tone of his voice alerted her. Had the events of the past few days heightened her perception? For Sophie knew with a breathtaking certainty that his relationship with this woman Alejandra was not one of innocent friendship.

'She's your mistress...' He didn't deny it. How could he? 'Since when?' she asked, her blue eyes piercing into him.

He was unable to look away and there was a long, heavy pause as he reluctantly answered the question. 'Since six months into my marriage,' he said eventually. He had told himself that he had no reason to lie to her, but even so he was surprised by her reaction.

She flung herself at him, blonde hair flying wildly, her nails flailing uselessly close to his impassive olive face as he caught hold of her wrists with a razor-sharp reflex.

'Rail at me to your heart's content,' he said. 'But do not mark me!'

'Why? Wouldn't Alejandra like it?'

'Stop it, Sophie!'

'Will you let go of me, please?'

'Once you stop trying to scratch me.'

'I won't scratch you.'

He let her go, but her nails came up again and he captured her once more. 'Ah, so you were lying, were you, *querida?*' he questioned softly. 'You promised that you would not attack me again.'

She stared at him, her heart thundering painfully in her breast. 'You…you spent *last night,* straight after the funeral, in the arms of another woman? Can that really be true, Luis?'

'You are the one demanding answers,' he observed quietly. 'Can I help it if they are ones you do not wish to hear?'

She felt like throwing something at him. Like pummeling her fists against that silk-covered chest. 'You…you…left your son sleeping while you made love to someone else?'

'Yes, my son *was* sleeping,' he hissed back. 'And safely in the care of Salvadora!'

'You unspeakable man!' she accused, rising shakily to her feet. 'Couldn't you have left a decent amount of time before you allowed your libido free range? Or maybe this is just par for the course? Maybe this is the kind of thing you used to get up to when Miranda was still alive!'

'*Collarse!*' he snapped, and when she stared at him in confusion he translated again into English. 'Keep your voice down!'

But she shook her head. 'What kind of man can possibly visit his mistress on the night of his wife's funeral?'

He felt all the fight go out of her and let her go, and this time she stumbled over to one of the chairs and sat down, her eyes dull.

'My God,' she breathed on a shuddering breath. 'No wonder Miranda was so unhappy!'

But Luis had had enough of her accusations and her judgements. He strode across the balcony towards her and levered her to her feet, his fingers biting into the soft, silken flesh of her arms as he gripped her. 'You know nothing of my marriage!' he accused.

'I know enough!'

'Will you be quiet, Sophie?'

'Never!'

He saw the defiant tremble of her mouth and something inside him snapped, like elastic which had been stretched to breaking point, and with a furious little moan of rage he pulled her hard against him, crushing his mouth down on hers even harder.

Anger and frustration and rage and a sense of injustice seemed to explode inside her like a devastating incendiary device as Sophie felt his lips capture hers as she had dreamed of them doing last night in bed. Only this time the dream was true. The fantasy real.

And, though it felt right, it was wrong. All wrong.

So why was she letting him kiss her—her breathing so weak and thready, but not so thready as to prevent the small, hungry sigh escaping from her lips? And why did the punishing pressure of his mouth make her feel as if she was melting? On fire with a need so fierce that she itched to burrow her hands up beneath the white silk of the shirt which did nothing to disguise the hard frame of his torso? As if no man had ever kissed her before? And, indeed, no man had.

Not like this.

Luis felt her arms wind up around his neck and the movement brought her soft, full breasts pressing into him, and his anger escalated, along with his desire. My God, he could ruck her skirt up and…and…

'*Dios!*' he ground out furiously. '*Mi Dios!*'

Through the hard, sweet pressure of his mouth and the aching of her swollen breasts Sophie felt the simmer of heat and hunger bubble up into an irrevocable burn.

Yet this was the man who had cheated on her cousin, who had visited his mistress only last night. A man whose sexuality was so explosively potent that it seemed he could reduce any woman he wanted into a compliant and uncomplaining partner, greedy for his kisses and his touch. Just as she was now.

She tore herself out of his arms to meet the hateful black mockery in his eyes but her breath was coming so quickly and so erratically that it took a moment before she could splutter out her own bitter accusation.

'That tells me everything I need to know!' she exploded. 'Just what kind of a man Miranda married. One who could kiss any woman so indiscriminately— just to shut her up!'

But Luis shook his head. It had not been indiscriminate. No, not at all. He had wanted to kiss her in the night and many times before that. And just recalling her softness and her warmth and the clean, innocent scent of her was enough to make him feel as though he could explode with frustration.

'That has been a long time in coming,' he said darkly. 'We both know that, so don't bother denying it to me, Sophie!'

Her breathing was still erratic, and her eyes blaz-

ing. 'Yes, I saw the way you looked at me the very
first time you saw me—as if you would like to drag
me off to the nearest bed!'

'And you did not look as if you would have objected if I had done,' he pointed out silkily.

The fact that he spoke nothing but the truth only
increased her sense of shame. 'I knew then what kind
of man Miranda was marrying—the kind of no-good
Don Juan who would leap on any woman who wanted
him to. If only I had told her,' she moaned. 'And if
she hadn't been pregnant then I would have done!'

'I think that this time you have pushed me too far,
Sophie,' he said in a voice which was dangerously
soft. He had tried to protect the memory of his late
wife out of respect, but he would not live a lie. Nor
let Sophie jump to false conclusions which would for-
ever damn him in her eyes; he had too much pride
for that. 'You leave me with no choice other than to
give you the true facts about my marriage.' His eyes
glittered with challenge. 'And only then shall you
have the right to judge me.'

'Knowing that it's in your interest to lie to me!'

He threw her a look of icy scorn. 'You think that
I would protect myself with lies? Never!'

And, oddly enough, the fierceness and the unmistakable aristocratic contempt in his voice actually
made her believe him. 'It is painful to recount,' he
began slowly. 'You see, in the beginning I liked your
cousin very much—she was funny and sweet and a
little bit crazy.' He sighed, wondering how many lives
would be lived differently if you were allowed a
glimpse into the future. 'We enjoyed a mutually sat-
isfying relationship.'

'How cold you make it sound, Luis!'

'Not cold—just how it was,' he contradicted. 'However different we might wish it to be. I am not a hypocrite, Sophie, you know that. And I would never admit to feelings that I did not have.' The warm morning sun beat down on him, but his skin felt cold. 'I was never "in love" with Miranda, Sophie,' he said softly. 'She knew that. I never made a secret of the fact. She was beautiful and sparky and we were good together. But she also knew that there was no long-term future in our relationship.'

She stared at him in frustration. 'But you *married* her! Why the hell did you marry her if you weren't in love with her?'

'I married her because, as you know, she was expecting my baby—a baby which was not planned...at least,' he added heavily, 'not by me.'

Sophie shook her head. She would not believe this; she wouldn't. 'If you're trying to tell me that Miranda deliberately got pregnant then I know that isn't so. She wasn't that desperate—*and* she was on the Pill! She told me!'

'What else did she tell you?'

'That it was true that the pregnancy wasn't planned, but that she'd had a stomach upset, and that—'

'Sophie!' he interrupted. 'I did not—do not—want to dishonour the memory of your cousin, but it was no accident when she became pregnant. Believe me. I was searching for some papers when I found her contraceptive pills. Untouched. I challenged her with it, and then she admitted that she had stopped taking them without telling me.'

'Oh, my God,' breathed Sophie. She remembered Miranda's excited chatter just after the wedding. She'd told Sophie how Luis was the most devastating man she had ever seen. How she had looked at him and thought, I've *got* to have him. Had she really planned it? The oldest trick in the book to get a man to marry you?

And with a sinking heart she guessed at the answer. 'She had a terrible childhood,' she said defensively. 'Her parents were never there for her—she was chronically insecure.'

'I am not blaming Miranda for her behaviour,' he said gently. 'I'm just telling you how it was.'

'But why still go ahead and marry her just because she was having your baby?' she demanded. 'Men don't have to do that any more, Luis. If you didn't love her you must have known from the outset that it wouldn't work.'

'I told you—because of my sense of responsibility. This was *my* child as well as hers! And Miranda did not want the baby to be born illegitimate. Indeed, neither did I. She decided that marriage could work and so did I. She wanted to enjoy the security which being married to me would bring, and which I was prepared to provide, and I would have the child which already my heart had begun to yearn for.'

'So it was a marriage of convenience, you mean?'

'Or a marriage of expedience,' he corrected.

'And were you honest with each other right from the start?' she demanded heatedly. 'Did you tell her that you couldn't possibly remain faithful and warn her that soon you would have to seek solace elsewhere? Was she prepared for you to have a mistress?'

There was another pause. 'No, she was not—and neither was I! I fully intended to honour my wedding vows, Sophie. I *am* a man of honour!' He narrowed his eyes as he remembered. 'And it would have been no hardship to remain faithful to a woman like Miranda. Marriage can be based on more than love, you know. Indeed, many cultures believe that it has a much better chance of survival if it is based on mutual respect, and trust.'

'But?' Because she sensed that there was a 'but' coming.

He chose his words carefully, not wanting to hurt her, but maybe hurt was the inevitable consequence of truth. 'I do not think that I offered Miranda the kind of life she was really seeking.'

'Oh, come on, Luis—she adored you!'

'No.' He shook his head resolutely. 'She liked what she thought I could offer her, but the reality fell far short of that. She adored the high life and the glamour of a playboy lover—which is what I was when we first met. Life as a wife and mother in La Rioja was not to her liking at all. She found the slower pace of life down here intolerable, and she wanted to live in Barcelona—she used to call it Paris by the sea—but that was not possible.'

'You could have compromised,' she pointed out. 'And gone there for weekends.'

'As we did. As we could have continued to do, even once Teo came along, but—as I once told you— a baby changes everything.'

'It doesn't have to,' she objected.

He sighed. 'That's what everyone who doesn't have one always says, but it does change things,

Sophie— more than you can know. When you have a baby then late nights out at clubs and sleeping until noon are no longer compatible.'

'That's what she did?'

'That's what she did,' he agreed evenly. 'In the end, she used to fly to Barcelona by herself, leaving Teo here while she partied into the small hours. I told her that if she continued to do so it was inevitable— only a matter of time—before we started leading separate lives. And so we did.'

'And that's when you found yourself a mistress?'

'No.' His expression became rueful. 'I did a very liberated and un-macho thing. I suggested we go for counselling. Miranda stuck to all of three sessions before she told me that she was having an affair. And *that* was when I began to look outside the marriage for what was being denied to me at home.'

She could hear the solemn ring of truth in his words, and in spite of everything her heart went out to him. 'Oh, Luis,' she whispered. 'It sounds awful. Why didn't you just get a divorce?'

He gave a bitter laugh. 'You think it's that easy? Maybe in England it is—but I had no intention of allowing Teo to be torn apart in some acrimonious custody battle. To have him living—at least for some of the time—with a mother who did not care for him properly. Many people have "empty" marriages, Sophie. It was tolerable.'

'And then she died.' She fixed him with a steady look, realising that the cardboard cut-out man she had thought he was simply did not exist; he was as complex as every other human being, perhaps even more so. And this rich, handsome and powerful man might not have given his heart to Miranda, but he had a strong sense of conscience, and of duty. 'I suppose in some way it must be a relief to be free from such an empty marriage.'

His mouth hardened. 'You think me such a black-hearted monster that I would wish the mother of my son dead?'

'But you didn't approve of her behaviour!'

'No, I didn't,' he agreed. 'And, yes, Sophie.' He sighed. 'I cannot deny that there was a certain amount of relief that there would be no more unhappiness. But, believe me, I felt guilt for feeling that.'

It must have been hard for him to admit that. But he had given her his honesty—didn't he deserve the same kind of honesty in return? 'I think I can understand it. None of us is safe from feelings we would prefer not to have,' she finished, with a note of bitter guilt in her voice.

'Thank you,' he said gravely.

She let out a long, sad sigh. Poor, sweet, misguided Miranda. Foolish Miranda. She had wanted Luis and, in a way, he had given her as much of himself that he was capable of giving—and she had thrown it all away in the mindless pursuit of life in the fast lane.

But with the knowledge that nothing was as simple as you thought it was came another, more frightening knowledge in its wake. She didn't want to think of Luis as an intrinsically good man, because if she did, wouldn't that make her want him even more? And he was not hers to have. With a history like theirs, he never could be.

Yes, that kiss had demonstrated that a powerful chemistry still existed between them, but she should not kid herself into thinking she was unique. When he kissed a woman it was probably always like that. What woman wouldn't go up in flames the instant a man like Luis touched her?

And besides, wasn't she forgetting something else? His behaviour during his marriage to Miranda might have been justified, but his behaviour this morning had not been.

'It doesn't change the fact that you kissed me just now, does it?' she demanded, conveniently forgetting that she had fantasised about just that during the night. 'And straight after your night of passion with your mistress! You must have little or no respect for either of us to do something like that!'

His mouth hardened, but this time he did nothing to correct her bitter allegations. The less she knew, the sooner she would be gone—and he *wanted* her gone. For what did he really know of Sophie Mills? Only that she had once gazed at him with a hunger which had temporarily sent him reeling, a hunger which had matched his own. And that her response to his kiss had spoken of a dangerous, sensual promise.

But that told him nothing of her true motives for being here. What did she really want? What was going on behind those bewitching blue eyes?

No, he needed her here like he needed a hole in the head.

He steeled himself. 'So what are we going to do about it, Sophie?' he drawled softly.

Sophie stared as the blaze from his eyes imprinted the memory of that kiss in her mind, so that for one horrifyingly tempting moment she thought that he meant…meant…

'You think…you think I want to carry on where we left off?' she demanded breathlessly.

His mouth hardened with tension and frustration. 'Is that what you would like, then?'

Part of her wanted to breathe that, yes, she would—more than she had ever wanted anything in her life. Knowing that if Luis led her up to bed right now he could give her nothing but pure and untold pleasure. Demonstrate to her that she was alive, and alive in the most fundamental way possible. And wasn't that what people often craved in the aftermath of death?

'Is it?' he prompted as he watched the slow wash of colour and the darkening of her eyes.

'I don't think I've ever received such an untempting offer in my life!'

'I wasn't making you an offer,' he countered insultingly. 'I was asking you a question. Though maybe the question that I *should* have asked was whether what has just happened has made you change your mind about staying?'

'Oh, now I see.' She glittered him a look. 'Is that why you did it? Because you thought I would be so outraged by your behaviour that I would storm out of here and leave without giving Teodoro a chance to get to know me? Well, if that's the case then I'm afraid you badly misjudged me, Luis!'

'You mean you still want to stay?'

She shook her head; all she knew was that she wanted to take Teo to England to meet his maternal grandmother—but instinct warned her that this was not the moment to ask him. 'I don't know if "want" is the word I would use. ''Need'' might be better. As I said, Teodoro needs to know that he has an alternative family.'

'Very well.' He gave her a look of cool appraisal, then shrugged. 'Finish your breakfast,' he said.

'As if nothing has happened?'

'And nothing has.' The black eyes lanced through her. 'Nor will it.'

'You mean you won't kiss me again?'

'Not through anger, no. There will be no need to silence you if you do not continue to make your harsh allegations against me, Sophie.' He curved his mouth into a cynical smile. 'Of course, if you invite me to then that is quite a different matter altogether.'

'Oh, don't worry, Luis—there's no chance of that!'

He lifted the coffee-pot and poured himself a cup. 'And if you intend to stay then I suggest that we should at least behave in a civil way towards each other. Do you think we could manage that, Sophie, to exist in harmony?'

Could they? Manage to ignore the niggling tensions which stubbornly wouldn't seem to go away?

He saw the indecision and reluctance on her face. 'You have an alternative suggestion?' he asked quietly. 'That we eat our meals in isolation? That we have no contact with each other during your stay? If that is to be the case, *querida,* then it means that you will see very little of your nephew. Whom you profess to want to get to know.'

'*Profess* to want to?' she echoed. 'Of course I want to get to know him! Why else do you think I am here?'

He shrugged and reached for a peach. 'I can think of a few reasons.'

'Such as?'

'Perhaps you wish to discover whether any of my fortune has been made over to your cousin, who in turn might have passed it on to you.'

Sophie sat down before her knees gave way. 'My God, how you constantly surprise me, Luis,' she said drily. 'There was I, thinking that your opinion of me couldn't get any lower, but how wrong I was! Sorry to disappoint you, but I am just not interested in your money!'

His eyes were lit from within, like ebony fire. 'No matter what we are thinking underneath, Sophie, you must force yourself to see reason,' he said softly. 'If my wife knew and accepted my relationship with Alejandra, then there is no earthly reason why it should offend *you*. Is there? And there is no point in us fighting. It matters nothing what I think of you, or you of me. For we are nothing to one another except in terms of our relationship with Teo, no matter how our bodies tell us differently.'

Strange how words could wound like arrows. 'Very well,' she agreed painfully. 'I'm sure I can manage to be civil for a few days.'

'Good. Oh, and before I forget,' he continued as he began to peel the peach with a small knife, until the skin fell into a voluptuous curl on his plate, 'I have a family wedding to attend in Madrid next weekend, and I shall be taking Teo with me. If you are still here you may wish to come along.'

'Seriously?'

'Why not?'

'Isn't that a little soon?' Surely even *he* would want to go through the motions of some kind of mourning ritual?

He continued to cut his peach, his knife piercing the soft, sweet flesh. 'Life goes on, Sophie, and especially life for my son. There will be family there, close family, who have not seen Teo for many months, and they will wish to embrace him and to comfort him.'

'And comfort you, too, I suppose,' said Sophie in a hollow voice. 'The grieving widower.'

He met her eyes with a calm look. 'It's up to you,' he said carelessly. 'Come if you wish, or stay behind, it matters little to me.'

'I—I don't have anything suitable to wear for a grand wedding.'

'I'm sure you will be able to find something—there are some very beautiful clothes available in the city,' he said, and gave a slow smile. 'I shall just have to take you shopping, won't I?'

It was a darkly proprietorial statement, the kind of careless statement that a man would make to his mistress, the kind of statement she could imagine him making to Alejandra, and it should have made her hackles rise.

So how come her heart had started racing as if in anticipation of some delicious, illicit pleasure?

CHAPTER SIX

Luis leaned forward. *'Palacio Santo Mauro, por favor!'*

The driver nodded. *'Sì, Don Luis.'*

The powerful limousine moved out of the airport towards the centre of Madrid and Luis settled back in his seat.

'Look at Madrid, Sophie,' he instructed softly. 'See her beauty for yourself.'

Sophie obediently stared out of the window, thinking that the city's beauty paled into insignificance when compared to the man beside her and reflecting on the turn-around in their relationship since he had told her the truth about his marriage.

Unbelievable, really.

There had been no more fighting, nor recriminations—both had been determinedly polite and courteous with each other, though they had warily circled one another, like two people determined to keep as much physical distance between themselves as possible.

And Luis had been right, Sophie recognised that now. She really was in no position to criticise him for having a mistress. It was his choice and his life and she was no part of it. But it still hurt more than it had any right to hurt whenever she thought about it, and so she tried not to think about it. Something made easier by the fact that, as far as she knew, he had paid no return visit to Alejandra—there had been no further nighttime trysts.

She guessed that he was waiting until she went back to England, and the return journey had been much on her mind, even though she had yet to come to a decision about when to leave. She knew that she could not stay indefinitely, but she still hadn't summoned up the courage to ask him about taking Teodoro with her. She was waiting for the right moment and that moment hadn't yet arrived. And she was still afraid of what his answer might be.

But she could not deny that the days before the wedding had been largely enjoyable days—almost too enjoyable, really.

In the mornings Luis went to work, leaving Sophie to help Salvadora with Teo, and now Sophie had gained Salvadora's trust, as well as Teo's affection—the older woman seemed eager to delegate more and more.

Not that Sophie minded—not a bit of it. Under Salvadora's watchful eye, she had begun teaching Teo to swim, and once Luis had come back from work unexpectedly early and found the two of them splashing around happily in the pool.

'What is this?' he had demanded, and Sophie had looked up, her wet hair plastered to her head and streams of water running down her face while Teo giggled against her cheek.

'I'm teaching Teo to swim!'

'Without my permission?' he questioned darkly.

'I won the county cup for breast-stroke!' she said. 'He's been perfectly safe with me!'

'I can see that for myself,' he responded softly,

trying to ignore the ache which her words had produced. Breast-stroke, indeed! Witch! 'But in future
you will clear any activities with me, Sophie, is that
understood?'

'Perfectly.' She nodded, and slid a little further
down into the turquoise water, the swimsuit suddenly
seeming just too revealing.

'Just in case you plan to take him rock-climbing,'
he finished laconically.

In the afternoons, after the siesta, Luis seemed determined to show Sophie as much of La Rioja and
the surrounding countryside as Teo's routine allowed.

And the more he showed her, the more she liked
it. She loved the region's peace and its natural beauty,
which made London seem very crowded and grey in
comparison. She saw for herself the clear, deep waters
of the wide River Ebro, the only river in Spain which
flowed down to the Mediterranean, its banks frilly
with vineyards and pinstriped with rows of garden
vegetables.

There were beautiful mountains in the Sierra de la
Demanda, and when she had said so he'd smiled, almost indulgently. 'Mmm, very beautiful, and high
enough to ski down. Do you ski, Sophie?'

She nodded. 'I'm completely addicted to it,' she
confessed.

'Me, too.'

She didn't want to discover the things that they had
in common. If only he had told her that he hated
skiing with a passion!

He had stopped the car so that they could look at
the breathtaking gullies of Rioja Baja. 'Look down

there,' he mused, his voice deepening. 'There dinosaurs once made the earth tremble—'

'Seriously?'

'They certainly did. Or at least left their curious tracks in a prehistoric bog, which petrified for posterity.'

He told her that, even today, tourists from all over the world came to the region to see for themselves the evidence of these huge and ancient beasts. It was a side of Spain she hadn't known existed.

'You thought we only had bulls?' he teased.

'I suppose I did,' she answered slowly.

'Shame on you, Sophie—for the gaps in your education!' But there was so much more than history that he wanted to teach her, knowing as well that it was forbidden. *She* was forbidden. And elusive and unknown, he reminded himself, and behind the wraparound shades he wore his eyes hardened.

One rare and deliciously cool afternoon, the three of them had travelled to Navarra's 'magic' mountain of Aralar, wooded with beech and rowan and hawthorn groves.

Sophie had unpacked the simple picnic and looked around, while Luis hoisted Teodoro up onto his shoulders for the best possible view while he told of the legend of San Miguel, and Sophie lay back and listened, mesmerised.

'It's a beautiful story,' she murmured when he had finished. 'And this is so beautiful, too.' She waved her hand to encompass the lush green landscape.

He raised his eyebrows. 'You thought it would be harsh and inhospitable?'

'A little,' she agreed, thinking that once she had

imagined him both these things, but he was neither. There was a sensitivity and a soulfulness to his character which did nothing to detract from his unquestionable masculinity and innate sensuality. It became easier to understand with each minute that passed just why Miranda had been so determined to have him.

And in the evenings, after supper, Sophie would retire to her room to catch up with her e-mails and to read through documents which Liam had forwarded to her.

Oliver had texted her and rung her and her reaction to the phone calls had brought her close to something like despair. She remembered how excited she had been at the prospect of dating him. But that excitement seemed to have evaporated into nothing more than mildly interested friendship. At least on her part. And she was perceptive enough to understand the reason why.

'When are you coming back, Sophie?' he'd asked. 'And having dinner with me?'

'I don't know. I haven't decided yet.'

'You know how much I want to take you out,' he murmured. 'I should have asked you ages ago, but I guess your reputation stopped me.'

'*What* reputation?' she laughed.

'Oh, you know—for being cool. Unapproachable.'

Cool? Unapproachable? She would bet a month's salary that Luis was not of the same opinion.

Just once, she had sat and drunk wine with him on the terrace, late into the night, with the moon huge as a dinner plate in the night sky. Around them the sounds of the cicadas had echoed in piercing yet restful chorus while she'd told him all about her company—her hopes and dreams for it and how close they looked to being fulfilled.

'I applaud you your ambition,' he said softly, and Sophie had to stifle a sigh. The perfect setting and the perfect man. Except that he wasn't perfect, she must keep telling herself that. And he certainly wasn't perfect for *her*.

The car glided down one of Madrid's main streets. It was beginning to feel too much like a holiday, she realised uncomfortably, and at that moment he moved, and the fabric of his trousers flattened distractingly over the hard shaft of his thighs.

Sophie swallowed. 'So tell me about the bride and groom,' she said quickly as the car began to pick up speed again.

He turned his head to look at her. 'What do you want to know?'

'Oh, the usual things. Something. Anything!' Anything to make her stop thinking about the mouth which had kissed her with such sweet, angry thoroughness.

If only the baby would wake up and occupy them! Divert her attention away from the watchful black glitter of his eyes. But Teodoro, who had been playful and communicative during the flight, was now sleeping happily.

'Ramon is a cousin of mine,' he replied. 'He is marrying Estrella, whom he has known for many years.'

'So does he love her?'

He turned his head to meet the challenge in her gaze, his eyes narrowing. He knew the subtext beneath her question—was his cousin's marriage going to replicate his own? 'Ramon loves Estrella with a passion,' he said quietly, and for the first time in his life he found himself envying someone.

'Well, I guess that's something.'

'Yes, it is—and she is far too fiery to contemplate ever sharing her *marido* with another woman.'

'And that's something, too!' she added drily.

'So you're a romantic at heart, are you, Sophie?' he mocked.

'I just believe that marriage should mean forsaking all others. That's what the vows say.'

'That's what they say all right,' he agreed evenly.

This was getting too compatible for comfort. 'So there'll be lots of your family at this wedding?'

'Yes. Lots. My parents. My sisters. Countless other cousins.'

'And the cream of Spanish aristocracy, I suppose?'

He inclined his head. 'Of course.'

He said it carelessly, as if it was the natural order of things, which she supposed it was. He was so sure of himself and his rarefied, exalted position in the world. And maybe that was the major part of his attraction. Would a woman look at him twice and lose her head over him if he were—say—a farmworker?

But then Sophie imagined the reality of that scenario, could picture it perfectly in her mind's eye. Luis engaged in hard physical labour, yes—that took no great leap of the imagination. His physique suggested that he could accomplish any such thing with ease. She could visualise tiny beads of sweat glimmering, burnishing the dark skin of his broad shoulders, the ripple of muscles as he worked the land, and her breath caught in her throat. A man like Luis would be desired by women no matter what he did.

'Won't they think it rather strange that you're bringing your wife's cousin along to a family wedding?'

'But it is precisely *because* you are family that they will accept it unthinkingly,' he murmured, noticing that her pupils had dilated and her lips had parted into a little pout, and he felt his body begin to harden with tension. 'The Spanish people put great value on a sense of family.'

She stared out of the window as the magnificent buildings of the capital passed them by, telling herself that she should consider herself lucky to be flown across Spain in the lap of luxury. But she didn't feel lucky. She felt...sad. Yes, sad, stupidly enough. Because soon she would leave this place and this man, and although she knew that it would only be for the best—part of her ached hopelessly to stay.

'You are excited to be in Madrid, Sophie?' questioned Luis softly, seeing the sudden tense set of her profile and wondering what had caused it.

'Kind of.'

'Oh, to be damned with faint praise! If Madrid were a woman she would now be shedding tears!' he murmured drily.

'Oh, I have nothing against the city.'

'Just your travelling companion, is that it?'

She turned to face him, arrested by the inky glitter of his eyes and the lush, kissable lines of his lips. 'Given the choice, I don't think I would have settled for a weekend away with you, no.'

'My ego is severely wounded,' he murmured.

'That makes a change.'

'Indeed it does,' he agreed gravely.

Sophie pressed her lips together, hating it when he teased her like that, or, rather, liking it too much, because it conjured up an intimacy which didn't really exist. They were just two people thrown together through circumstance and making the best of an awkward situation.

But at the moment it didn't feel like an awkward situation. She felt as excited as a schoolgirl on her first trip abroad—being with him and Teo in a glamorous city, with the prospect of staying at one of Spain's finest hotels.

Perhaps a more sensible woman would have refused to accompany him on this trip, but what would have been the point of that? To wander aimlessly around the beautiful villa on her own, with Teodoro miles away—when getting to know him was her sole reason for being here? And as she kept telling herself, she couldn't stay on indefinitely...

Liam and the others were coping perfectly well back at the office, but the fact remained that she had a pivotal role in the company and she could not leave it unfilled indefinitely while she luxuriated in Spain.

As if on cue, the mobile phone in her bag rang, and she heard Luis click his tongue impatiently against the roof of his mouth.

'Don't you ever turn that thing off?' he drawled.

'There wouldn't be a lot of point in having a mobile phone if people can't reach me on it, would there?' she replied serenely, clicking the connection and reading the name which flashed up on the screen. 'Liam! Hi! What's happening?'

Luis raised his eyebrows as he smoothed back a black curl from Teo's cheek. She had told him that Liam was her partner—but perhaps her 'partner' wanted more than a business arrangement, judging from the amount of times he seemed to ring her!

And what of this Oliver—who also seemed very fond of phone calls and sending her a series of text messages.

What, he mused, would either man say if he knew how much she was trying to fight her attraction towards him? An attraction made all the more obvious by the way she constantly tried to hide it. From herself, he suspected, just as much as from him.

He wondered if she knew how transparent her face could be. If she was aware that her pupils always darkened when their eyes met, only to be followed by cheeks being flushed by a telltale guilty pink, as if she was afraid that he could read her thoughts.

Not her thoughts, no; at least, not always. But her body, yes—that was easy enough to read. And a lifetime of being finely tuned to the desires of women convinced Luis that Sophie was by no means immune to him.

'No, I'm in Madrid,' she was saying. 'With Luis.'

'*Madrid?*' Liam echoed. 'You mean you're at the airport? Does that mean you're coming home?'

'Er—no. Not yet. I'm…I'm actually on my way to a family wedding.'

There was a short, disbelieving silence. 'With *him?*'

Sophie shot a glance at Luis's profile, but even though he could hear every word she was saying it was as expressionless as if it had been carved from some golden-olive marble. She watched as he absently smoothed the dark curls of the sleeping child.

'That's right,' she agreed, thinking that as a father he couldn't be faulted. He was a wonderful father.

'Are you listening, Sophie?' questioned Liam, and to her horror she realised that she had switched off, letting her thoughts run away—and lately they seemed to be running in a very predictable direction indeed.

'I thought the whole point of you going over there was to be with your nephew,' he objected. 'Not gallivanting around the place with a man you're supposed to despise.'

'Teodoro's with us.'

'That's not what I meant—'

'Listen, Liam, I can't really talk now,' she said rather pointedly, because Luis's mouth had hardened into a brief, hard smile and she was worried that Liam might say something *really* insulting about him and that he might hear. 'Was there something in particular you wanted to speak to me about?'

'What? Oh, yeah. It's Ted Jacobs—'

'I e-mailed him first thing!'

'He wants to see you.'

'Well, he *can't!*'

'But he said—'

'Listen, Liam,' she interrupted, because Teodoro was now beginning to stir, 'you're perfectly capable of dealing with Ted yourself.'

'Yeah, but he prefers you.'

'I know he does,' she sighed. 'But you'll just have to explain to him what's happened. I need to be here; my nephew needs me.'

'And what about Luis?' questioned Liam slowly. 'Does he need you, too? Sounds to me like you're conveniently slotting in where your cousin left off, Sophie. Cosy, cosy, cosy! Is that it?'

If only he knew that Miranda had spent the majority of her time at the opposite end of the country! Sophie knew Liam was only asking out of concern for her, but she couldn't really start explaining patiently to Liam that Luis hardly needed a replacement wife—not when he had a mistress waiting patiently in the wings.

'Ring me on Monday,' she sighed. 'I'll be back from Madrid by then! OK?'

'OK,' he echoed. 'I'll talk to you on Monday. Have a good time.' But he didn't sound as though he meant it.

She broke the connection to find Luis looking at her, and the deep voice was full of a lazy amusement which matched the expression in his eyes. 'So, they cannot cope without you?'

'I suppose I should be flattered that they miss me when I'm not there.'

'But you are not flattered?' he observed.

She stole a look across to where Teodoro's eyelashes were just beginning to flutter. Funny how you could suddenly find you were changing your mind about certain things. Sophie had two god-daughters, whom she adored, but she had never been one of those women who put having a baby at the top of their wish-list.

Yet the time she had been spending with Teo had been a real eye-opener. She had discovered that cajoling a smile out of a toddling infant could be just as rewarding as landing a big business deal.

Or maybe it was just Teo himself, and the effect he had on her. Dreamily she smiled down at his sleeping head, until she remembered that Luis had been talking to her, and she looked up to find his black eyes sizzling into her.

'Not particularly flattered, no,' she said, dragging her thoughts back to the present. 'It makes me wonder if I haven't bothered to delegate effectively if they can't do without me for a couple of weeks. Or maybe we should just think seriously about taking someone else on. It had crossed my mind that the staff quota hasn't kept up with company expansion.'

In the evenings he had heard the blip of her computer while she worked in her room. 'You work hard,' he commented.

'Well, so do you.'

'Not too much just lately,' he answered flatly.

'You've had your hands full with Teo.'

'Yes.' He gave a wry glance at his son. And not just with Teo, with Sophie, too. Mountain picnics weren't supposed to be on his agenda. He had tried telling himself that their excursions were solely for his son's benefit—except that wouldn't have quite been the truth, because he enjoyed showing her his country. And, let's face it, he thought, she has proved to be a very enthusiastic and decorative recipient.

'And the vineyards haven't ground to a halt without you, have they?' she teased.

He laughed. 'Not yet they haven't.'

'Nobody's indispensable, Luis. Not even you.'

'Nor you either,' he mused.

Teo woke up then and jabbed a finger against his father's mouth and giggled—as if wanting his father to laugh some more—and the car glided to a halt in front of a vast building.

A uniformed doorman pulled the door open and Sophie looked up at the magnificent façade. 'Good heavens,' she said faintly. 'Is this where we'll be staying?'

'Not just us. Most of the family have taken rooms. Do you like it, Sophie?'

Like it? How could she not? 'It's lovely.'

'Just wait until you see the interior,' he promised.

He was as good as his word. Inside was a wood-lined interior of mirrors and paintings, and enormous potted palms. The vaulted ceiling seemed to go on for ever and the air was cooled by old-fashioned fans.

It was difficult not to be slightly overawed at such an unashamedly luxurious place, but Teodoro was grizzling by now, squirming in his father's arms while Luis was speaking in rapid and incomprehensible Spanish to the receptionist, a whole mass of baby equipment at his feet.

'Come, Teo,' whispered Sophie, holding her arms out tentatively towards him. 'Come to Sophie.' And to her delight he wriggled inside them, snuggling up comfortably against her breasts. She buried her nose in the sweet fragrance of his hair and held him very tight, and Teo giggled and began to play with her hair.

Unseen, Luis had watched the whole little scene, and his dark eyes narrowed. He was reluctantly moved by the way she was around his son. Her reaction was not feigned; he could tell that—and Teo would have seen through it if it had been. Children could always tell whether affection was genuine.

It perplexed him.

It was unusual for a woman of her independence to invest so much time and emotion and commitment in a child who would never be more than on the periphery of her life.

So why? Was it simply love and loyalty to her cousin which made her act in this way, or did she have an ulterior motive? Some hidden agenda which might later become clear? But the bellboy was standing waiting and Luis nodded. Now was not the time to dwell on 'what ifs' which might never happen.

'Come, Sophie,' he said softly. 'They will show us to our rooms.'

The rooms were more like individual suites of the penthouse variety.

'All this, just for me?' asked Sophie as she stood in the middle of a floor the size of a ballroom, still holding Teo in her arms and resisting the urge to dance around with him.

'You sound like a little girl,' he murmured, watching her uninhibited pleasure as she looked around the room.

'I *feel* like a little girl, let loose in the sweet shop!'

He imagined her in pigtails and had to stifle a groan as she bent and put Teo gently down on the carpet and he immediately began to crawl.

'Where will he sleep?' she asked him.

'I have arranged to have a cot in my room.' He pointed to a door at the far end of the room. 'Through there.'

Sophie swallowed. 'A-adjoining rooms?'

'It's a family suite—there is usually a connecting door.' His eyes glittered with a mocking challenge. 'Why, does it bother you?'

It most certainly did. The thought of such a thin divide between them. Of Luis in bed only yards away. At least back at the hacienda there had been a whole long corridor between them, and the knowledge that Salvadora and Pirro were also in the house acting as unseen chaperons.

But she met his eyes with a gaze as coolly mocking as his own. 'Not at all. Should it?'

A small smile curved the edges of his lips. She was lying. She knew it and he knew it. How would she respond if he challenged her?

But Teo had now set off at speed around the room, and already Luis could see several objects which needed to be moved out of reach of an inquisitive little hand.

He picked up the bin just as Sophie whisked away the bowl of complimentary sweets.

'I think we'll lose the candy,' she said, and reached up to put it safely away on the top of a bureau. 'Er—Luis.'

'Mmm?' He had been watching the lithe movement of her body as she stretched up. She had twisted her hair up and pinned it to the top of her head, leaving her long neck bare, save for a stray silken wisp, and he recalled the night he had walked into her bedroom, the way her hair had streamed down over her breasts, thick as honey.

She turned round, and wrinkled her nose as she picked Teo up. 'I think Teo needs changing. Do you want me to do it?'

He frowned. 'You think I cannot?'

'I don't know. Can you? I notice that you usually leave that side of things to Salvadora.'

'She seems happy enough to do it.'

'She probably can't imagine the sight of Don Luis de la Camara doing such a thing. Women's work,' she added drily.

'But you think it's a man's work, too?'

'Of course I do! Baby care has to be shared—you can't just delegate the less pleasant parts and keep all the best bits for yourself, otherwise how would you ever bond with him properly?' She smiled up at him, enjoying the rare moment of perplexity which made him look disconcertingly approachable. 'Would you like me to show you how?'

The perplexity vanished and was replaced with a look of outrage. 'I do not need lessons from you, Sophie!' he growled.

'You've done it before, have you?' she questioned doubtfully.

No, he hadn't. But, by the hand of God, surely it could not be difficult to change a nappy?

It appeared that it was.

Which was why Luis's mother found her son kneeling on the ground, trying to attach a clean nappy to a wriggling Teo, with Sophie, having fought desperately hard not to laugh, eventually losing the battle and dissolving into a fit of the giggles.

'You're hopeless!'

'Por Dios!' he exclaimed.

'Luis?'

He turned his head and saw his mother standing at

the door, her elegant features set into a look of be-musement. *'Buenos dias, Madre!'*

'Here.' Sophie crouched down beside him. 'Let me. You go and greet your mother.'

He sizzled her a frustrated stare. 'You will teach me later,' he murmured, and then he was on his feet, embracing his mother as they kissed on both cheeks.

'You did not bring Salvadora with you?' questioned his mother in Spanish.

He shook his head. 'She is getting old, Madre. And besides, Sophie said that it would do me good to have sole responsibility for him.'

'Oh, *did* she?' asked his mother, her dark eyes looking questioningly at her son. But by then Sophie had scooped up a happy and contented child and was holding him out towards his grandmother, who immediately took him and began to rain kisses on his ebony curls.

'My beautiful, beautiful grandson!' she exclaimed as Teo began to play with her exquisite pearl necklace.

'Isn't he?' Luis smiled and then began to speak in English. 'Mother, I need to take Sophie shopping to buy a dress to wear for the wedding—'

His mother smiled. 'And you want to leave Teo with me, is that it?'

'You don't mind?'

'Mind? Leave him with me for a week if you wish! Even longer!'

He glanced down at his watch. 'We'd better get going if we're going to make it in time.'

He hailed a cab outside and ordered it to drive to

the Salamanca region, where the city's finest shops were situated.

'Do you think your mother minds me being here?' asked Sophie as the door of an upmarket shop slid open. 'You said she wouldn't.'

'No, I don't think so,' he murmured. 'Why should she?'

'I just thought she looked at me a little strangely back there.'

He suspected that the look had something to do with his revelation that Sophie had offered him advice. And that he had taken it. 'It was probably the sight of her oldest son on his knees, changing a nappy,' he commented wryly. 'Come, now, Sophie, and tell the young lady what it is you are looking for.'

The clothes were out of this world, and Sophie was torn between an ice-blue floor-length sheath in clinging silk, with a matching coat which could be worn in the church, and a starker, more chic outfit in sophisticated grey.

'I can't decide! Which?' She turned to the salesgirl.

'Turn around,' came Luis's deep, velvety voice.

Slowly she twirled, acutely aware of the dark eyes appraising her.

'Get the blue,' he said carelessly, though his mouth was dry with desire. 'It matches your eyes.' And the dress clung like a second skin.

But when Sophie emerged from the changing room it was to find Luis charging the outfit to his account.

'What the hell do you think you're doing?'

'What does it look like, *querida?*'

'I am perfectly able to buy my own clothes!'

'But it is an unexpected expense. You were not expecting to have to purchase something of this value. Come, Sophie, let me buy it for you.'

'No! Definitely not!'

His black eyes glittered. 'I can afford it!'

'I know you can, and so can I! Here—' With a polite smile she gently removed his credit card from the fingers of the bemused sales assistant, and replaced it with one of her own.

There was a moment of highly charged silence. 'You are very stubborn, *querida*,' he said silkily.

'You're pretty stubborn yourself,' she returned. 'Or is it just that no woman has ever turned down a gift from you before?'

'But why should they?' he asked seriously. 'When I am happy to give it?'

Sophie stared at him. Had he never been with a woman who tried to meet him on equal terms? 'It's to do with something called pride, Luis,' she said quietly.

Pride.

Orgullo.

He gave a cynical half-smile. It was not a word he usually associated with the women in his life. Women wanted him; they had always wanted him—and to that end a gift would have been seen as a symbol of their importance. So why was Sophie Mills looking at him with such disdainful scorn?

'Why do you refuse?' he husked as the salesgirl turned away to wrap up the outfit.

'Because it would make me feel like a kept woman!'

He guessed that now was not the time to point out

that 'kept' women usually provided favours in return
for gifts—because with that mutinous look on her
face he could not trust her not to deliver an almighty
ringing slap to his cheek in the middle of the department store!

He shrugged in impatient and uncharacteristic capitulation. 'Very well! You may pay for it if you insist!'

'Oh, thank you very much,' she returned sarcasti-
cally. 'I fully intend to.'

He itched to subdue her in a way which would have
her sighingly accept his offer. To have her make such
a scene and to refuse his offer in front of the sales
assistant! She spoke of pride—did she not consider
that she had offended his own masculine pride?

He simmered quietly in the car on the ride back to
the hotel and Sophie sighed as she looked at his unforgiving profile.

'Of course, if you're going to be in a bad mood for
the rest of the day—'

'Why should I be in a bad mood?' he questioned
airily.

'Because you didn't get your own way! I thought
that we were emphatically *not* going to judge each
other during this trip. So humour me in my independence, won't you, Luis?'

He stared into her eyes and met the glint of amusement there. 'Very well, stubborn Sophie,' he sighed.
'The subject is closed, forgotten. Now sit back and
enjoy the city.'

CHAPTER SEVEN

THERE was only just enough time left for Sophie to shower and change for the wedding, and she had just finished applying a final slick of lipstick when Luis knocked on her door.

'Sophie? Are you ready?'

A final glance in the mirror and Sophie nodded. She would do. She would have to. 'Yes. Come in!'

Carrying Teo, Luis entered the room, and he stilled when he caught that first sight of her, his black eyes narrowing like those of some jungle cat who had stumbled upon some unknown predator.

Sophie swallowed and dabbed her fingertips to her face. Had she inadvertently missed her lashes and smudged mascara all over her cheek? 'Is something wrong?'

Wrong? *Madre de Dios!* Had anything ever looked more right? The woman looked like a goddess brought to golden and gleaming life. Luis felt a pulse begin to beat heavily in his temple. And even more heavily in his groin. He shook his head. 'You're wearing make-up,' he commented throatily.

'Well, of course I'm wearing make-up! I'm going to have to stand next to numerous beautiful members of the Spanish aristocracy, so I have to look my best.'

'But you don't usually bother.'

'I know. Only for special occasions. It always

113

seems slightly mad to me to spend ages slapping the stuff on, only to have to take it off again!'

And the delicacy of her features and the huge blue eyes meant that, unlike most women, she could get away with the scrubbed look. But with make-up... He sucked in a raw breath of longing... She looked utterly magnificent!

Her eyes seemed to dominate her face, the darkening of the mascara emphasising their saucer-shape, while the shiny lipstick made her mouth all provocative pout. Her skin gleamed, softly golden, smooth as silk and just as sensual.

And the dress...

Luis couldn't keep his eyes off it.

The sensual fabric of the silk clung like syrup to her breasts and her hips, making the most of their slender curves. Sweet heaven! he thought heatedly. If it had been anyone else but Sophie, he might have suggested caressingly that she let her hair down, but that was most definitely not within his remit.

'You look extremely beautiful, *querida*,' he said haltingly.

So did he, if the word beauty could be applied to such an unequivocally masculine man. And somehow, yes, it could, for beauty could be angular and lean and hard as well as soft and luscious and curved.

She couldn't stop her eyes from drinking in the vision he made, his lean body defined by the formal cut of the dark suit, drawing attention to the length of his legs and the narrow jut of his hips. He must have just shaved, because for once the strong curve of his jaw was without its usual faint shadowing and the thick black hair gleamed with tiny droplets of water, fresh from the shower.

It took an almighty effort, but somehow she dragged her eyes away from him to Teo, resplendent in a snowy-white sailor-suit trimmed with navy blue. 'And you look utterly gorgeous, Teo,' she whispered. 'What a handsome boy!'

Teo cooed and suddenly the huge room seemed far too small, and, God-forbid him, Luis wished that they were alone, unbearably tempted to take her into his arms, and to kiss the soft pink lips clean of all that lipstick. He swallowed.

'Come. Let us go,' he said thickly.

A car was waiting to take them to the ancient flower-filled church and Sophie could feel curious eyes on them as they walked up the aisle to take their places with his family. Did she imagine it, or could she hear whispered voices murmuring in Spanish as they entered the church? Were they wondering who was the blonde woman who accompanied the Don and his young son?

It was an emotional ceremony, but then weddings were supposed to be emotional, weren't they? Except for Miranda's, Sophie realised suddenly. A colourless register office on a hot summer day, with Miranda pale and wilting and newly pregnant. But there had been an unmistakable note of triumph as she had made her vows and Luis's accented response had been faultless. But without passion.

Not like this. The bride's voice shook as she made her vows and the look of adoration in her new husband's eyes made Sophie feel breathless with a wishful kind of envy.

I want that too, she realised. If ever I marry it must be to a man who loves me with that fierce kind of passion. I want love, she thought wistfully. Real, enduring love. The kind of love which could move mountains.

And the man who stood beside her could never give her that. Never in a million years.

She glanced over at Teo, who had been surprisingly quiet and was now sucking his thumb as the choir gave a soulful rendition of some haunting Spanish hymn.

He was growing to know her, yes, and even to like her—but how long would it take before Luis would entrust Teo into her care and allow her to take the child to England?

She was going to have to discuss it, and soon, she decided as she stood up for the final blessing.

The reception was held in the ballroom of the hotel and was the most lavish occasion that Sophie had ever been to. They were serving exquisite regional delicacies and fine de la Camara wines, and the overpowering scent of the white lilies which adorned the room was decadently heady.

Teo was whisked from relative to relative while Luis introduced Sophie to various aunts, cousins and uncles.

Their eyes were curious enough, but they asked no questions about her presence—she supposed that generations of aristocratic breeding kept their conversation strictly neutral, though what they were thinking was anyone's guess.

And what was Luis thinking, as female after beautiful female sought his attention? His eyes gave nothing away, other than a slightly indulgent inky glitter as one woman after another attempted to monopolise him.

Then the music began. Soft, beguiling strings to lure people onto the dance floor. The bride and groom. Parents. Cousins. A middle-aged uncle whirling Teo around and an exquisite young Spanish woman who glanced up at Luis with eager shyness. He nodded, almost imperceptibly, as he took her into his arms.

'Such a—handsome couple they make,' murmured one of Luis's aunts in halting English as they danced past.

'Don't they?' Sophie agreed, but her heart was racing and she cursed the stupid, sharp and unrealistic pang of jealousy. He was not hers to be jealous of. Shaking her head at her own weakness, she went over to fetch herself a glass of water, quite prepared to be a wallflower but not prepared to watch while Luis moved with such careless grace with a succession of different women in his arms.

She sat it out for three numbers, sheltering behind a large potted plant, until she heard his deep, rich voice penetrating her mixed-up thoughts and felt herself tremble.

'Soph-ie?'

She glanced up and the watchful blaze from his black eyes dazzled her.

'Why are you hiding over here?' he asked her softly.

She forced a smile. 'I didn't hide well enough, did I, for you found me easily enough?'

He sat down in the chair beside her. 'Was that your intention, then, Sophie—to hide from me?'

She wondered what he would say if she told him the truth, that it hurt, it actually physically *hurt* to see another woman in his arms.

'I just wanted to rest my feet,' she lied.

'And now that you have rested them...' he allowed his gaze to travel to where the sexy little shoes rested beneath two such delicate ankles; she wore no stockings and he found himself wanting to remove the shoes, to massage the smooth and gleaming flesh, to rub the nub of his thumb round and around the instep of her sole '...are you going to dance with me?'

'I—I don't think that's such a good idea.'

'Oh?'

'People might think it rather strange—and I have no desire—' liar! '—no wish to monopolise you,' she breathed. 'Come on, Luis—there are any number of women here who must be dying for you to ask them.'

'But I am asking you, Sophie,' he persisted. 'And people will think it strange indeed if the Don does not dance with the woman who is his guest here. Come, Sophie—it is *my* wish. And if you do not desire—' he smiled as his voice lingered deliberately on the word '—to be discourteous you will do me the honour of dancing with me.'

She had never been asked to dance in quite such an irresistible way, but then she had never been asked to dance with a man quite so irresistible as Luis. It is courtesy, she reminded herself as he drew her into his arms. Simply courtesy.

But oh, the reality was heartachingly different. The sensation of being in his arms, with his hands resting

lightly on her hips was such a delicious experience
that she could scarcely breathe.

He pulled her against him and instantly his head
was full of the scent of lilac. His fingers splayed possessively at the indentation of her narrow waist, the
thin fabric of her dress making her seem outrageously
accessible, almost as if he could feel her skin itself.
But he wanted her closer, and closer still, and as he
turned her round he drew her even tighter, watching
her reaction and seeing the startled dilatation of her
eyes as she made first contact with the inevitable evidence of how much he wanted her.

'Luis,' she said weakly.

'*Sì, querida?* You like to dance with me?'

She liked it more than was decent, but wasn't it
just tantalising her to an unbearable pitch? Did he
know what he was doing to her? He was so hard, and
so magnificently unashamed of his arousal. Did every
other woman he had danced with have the same effect
on him? And were they, in turn, just longing to press
themselves even harder against the jut of his hips and
to feel the very cradle of his masculinity?

'You move very well.' She swallowed, praying that
this wanting would go away.

He stifled a groan of frustration. So, sweet tor-
ment—so did she move very well. How much longer
could he endure such temptation, and how long she?

She was starting to care, Sophie realised, and to
care too deeply, for she wanted more than just his
body—she wanted to see deep into his quick and
clever mind, to find out for herself just what made
Luis de la Camara really tick. But such wanting
would bring her nothing. He already had a mistress,

she reminded herself painfully, and so what the hell was he doing dancing with *her* like this?

The longer she stayed, the stronger the possibility that she would fall completely under his spell, and there was no future in it, no future at all. Could she bear that?

No, she could not. It was time to leave. And the sooner the better. 'I've had enough of dancing now,' she said shakily.

And so had he. Much more and he would find it impossible not to heatedly move his fingers across the satin surface of her back, and then to let them curve round to cup the luscious swell of her breasts.

He let his hands fall from her waist. 'We will find Teo,' he said flatly.

She knew that she could not put off telling him any longer, but she waited until later, when they were back in their rooms and a tired but happy Teo had been put to bed.

She rapped lightly on his door.

Luis was just taking off his cuff-links and trying to shake off the deep ache of frustration which had not left him all evening.

'Come in!'

The door opened and he turned around to see Sophie standing silhouetted in the doorway and his breath caught in his throat. He saw that she had let her hair down and that it gleamed in silken and golden array around her shoulders, and his eyes narrowed. Did she not know the danger in which she placed herself, or was she unaware that the light from behind her had turned the dress almost transparent, outlining the long, slender length of her legs?

Through the bodice he could see the tightened nubs of her nipples and the frustration inside him built up into an unbearable pitch.

He could hear his voice sounding unfamiliarly thick. *'Sì?'*

She stood in the doorway uncertainly. It was too intimate—far too intimate—to catch him in the act of undressing. How could she speak—when the words caught like dry pebbles in her throat? How *did* she? 'May I—may I speak to you for a moment, please?'

He glanced down at the sleeping child, and nodded, even though the words which must next be spoken sent all kinds of fantasies exploding into his mind's eye. 'But next door, in your bedroom,' he grated. 'Where Teo will not be disturbed.'

She nodded, her heart crashing against her ribs as he followed her into the room. It was like every dream she'd ever had come true. Except that it wasn't—it was going to be nothing more than a matter-of-fact talk which was long overdue.

Luis was almost driven crazy by the sight of her bottom as she walked in front of him. Sweet heaven—but the faint hint of a thong clearly outlined as the silk stretched over each high, curved buttock would have stretched any man's endurance.

And he knew then that he could not sleep, nor even live with himself if he did not do this...

'Luis!' she cried as with a sudden, unexpected movement he caught her in his arms and turned her around to face him, his mouth hovering deliciously close to hers. 'What are you doing?'

'What we have both wanted me to do all night,' he said unsteadily. 'To kiss you.'

'You promised that you would—'

'I promised that I would not kiss you in anger,' he agreed unsteadily. 'But there is no anger in me now, *querida*. Nor in you. I see nothing but sweet invitation in your eyes, and what kind of a man would I be if I ignored that delicious, silent message?'

It means nothing, she told herself. Just lust, that was all. But it didn't seem to make any difference, because nothing could have stopped her from succumbing to the raw passion which gleamed from his eyes, and the provocative promise of his parted lips. He bent his mouth to hers, her own automatically opening beneath his, the sharp tang of longing made satisfied and yet more hungry still with that first sweet contact.

She clung to him helplessly as he kissed her with a thoroughness which made her melt even further against his lean body, and with a groan he cupped her breasts and Sophie's knees threatened to give way.

'*Querida,*' he breathed as he incited a tiny nipple with the tip of his thumb.

She was on fire where he touched her with mind-blowing provocation. His hard thigh was pushing insistently against her and she felt her own legs parting of their own volition. And now he was impatiently rucking up the silky fabric of her dress, his fingertips feeling heated as they tiptoed over the cool flesh of her inner thigh. She squirmed in anticipation, wanting to beg him to touch her, and once he touched her…

Somewhere deep in the recesses of her mind, cold and inescapable logic acted like a bucket of icy water tipped all over her. She had to stop this and she had to stop it now, before it went too far—before either

of them was unable to stop. How could she forget
that this cold-hearted and distant man was a philan-
derer—and one who had made Miranda's life a misery?

Her body screaming out its protest, she stopped
kissing him and pushed his hand away from her panties, trying to ignore the frowning look of frustration
on his face and wondering if she looked just the same.

'Have a few days of abstinence from *Alejandra*
made you long for a substitute mistress?' she gasped
as she smoothed her dress down. 'If she's not around,
then will anyone do?'

He shook his dark head impatiently. 'Alejandra is
not my mistress!'

'As of when? As of now? You had sex with her
on the night of the funeral. Surely you haven't forgotten *that?*'

'I did not have sex with her!' he ground out.

'Then why did you rush off to see her? To play
backgammon?'

Did she imagine that he was capable of giving
nothing other than sexual pleasure? he wondered
heatedly. 'I went to see Alejandra because I realised
that our relationship was over.'

'Convenient timing,' she volunteered drily.

'Not really.' He shook his dark head. 'Death forces
you to confront reality—and the reality was that
Alejandra was demanding far more than I was prepared to give her.'

'And what was that?' she questioned unsteadily.

He let out a heavy sigh. 'Our affair was never
meant to be more than that—but she had mistakenly
come to believe that because I was now ''free'' there

was no obstacle standing in our way. And that we would soon be a couple—in every sense of the word.'

'She wanted to marry you?'

He gave an odd kind of smile. 'Alejandra has sensibilities, Sophie,' he said softly. 'And marriage was not actually mentioned, but, yes, I believe that was her true wish.'

So that was why he had dumped her—because she was getting too demanding, and Luis was not the kind of man who could cope with emotional demands.

She felt the slow sizzle of anger. Was this the way he treated all his mistresses? Discarding them once they were no longer satisfied with their tiny and limited role in his life?

And here he was, trying to make love to *her*— while she, stupid fool that she was, had very nearly fallen captive in his sensual snare!

She had to get out—and get out *now!*

'You insult me with your attempt to make love to me,' she said icily. 'And you treat women as second-class citizens! I'm going back to England, Luis—and I want to take Teodoro with me!'

CHAPTER EIGHT

LUIS'S eyes narrowed, all his frustrated desire for her melting away in the light of her unbelievable statement.

'Say that again,' he purred dangerously.

'I want to take Teo back to England. My grandmother wishes to meet him.'

'You will take Teo nowhere!' he snapped.

'I don't mean permanently—'

'Temporarily isn't even an option!' he said furiously. 'How dare you even suggest it?'

Oh, God—why had she stumbled it out so baldly? 'Please, Luis—'

But he hardened his heart against the appeal in her eyes. His instincts had told him not to trust her but he had let his desire dictate that those instincts go unheeded. 'What kind of fool are you, Sophie—to think that I would allow you to remove my son from his native land? Is it your intention to keep him there? To gain custody of him for yourself? Is that it, Sophie? Has that been your plan all along?'

'No, of course it hasn't!'

'There is no ''of course'' about it! We both know how notoriously difficult it is to extradite a child from another country,' he cut across her, still in that same, steely voice. 'You must be crazy if you thought that I would agree to such a scheme!'

Maybe she was. Too crazy for her own good.

Minutes ago she had actually been contemplating falling into bed with him—the man who could break her heart and chew it up and spit it out again. And instead of throwing herself on his mercy, of explaining her grandmother's request, she had issued what had sounded like an unreasonable demand. Had she really imagined that because he had proved to be a delightful partner over the last few days he would allow her to get on an aeroplane with his beloved son?

'Listen, maybe I phrased it badly—'

'Badly, perhaps—but at least truthfully,' he ground out. 'Is that why you've been so sweet and approachable lately, I wonder—because you wanted to lull me, to lure me into agreeing? Is that why you responded so beautifully in my arms while we danced tonight? Did you think that you might even make love to me, to lure me further still, to procure exactly what you wanted? Only at the last moment you couldn't go through with it, could you? Could not bring yourself to make love to a man you despise, no matter how much you wanted to get your hands on Teo?'

'Luis! You can't possibly believe that!'

'Oh, but I can! You have never made any secret of your real feelings for me—you just happen to be a consummate enough actress to be able to disguise them for a while.' His eyes glittered with rage. 'Perhaps that is also the reason why you were so accommodating towards my son?'

That hurt more than anything else he had said so far. 'Y-you honestly think that I manipulated Teo for my own ends?'

'How the hell do I know?'

She tried one last time. 'Luis, please—'

'Oh, spare me your pleas!'

She stared at him, this black-eyed stranger who was almost unrecognisable as the man who had just kissed her with such sweet, wild passion. 'And that is your final answer?'

'It is,' he agreed implacably.

'Then there is nothing more to be said.'

'No,' he agreed tightly. 'Not a single word.' His black eyes seared into her one last time, and then, with a final hardening of his mouth, he turned and left the room without another word.

Sleep was a long time in coming and Sophie awoke late to find that Luis was already up and dressed. He had left her a curt note to say that he had taken Teo downstairs for breakfast.

She showered and dressed and made her way to the dining room, seeing him seated at the far end of the room, his dark head bent and his mouth smiling as he spooned something into Teo's mouth.

Did he hear her footfall, or did he simply sense her presence in the room? Because he looked up as she approached, and his face grew hard and stony.

'Sit down, Sophie,' he said, the glitter in his eyes belying the courtesy of his words. 'Did you sleep well?'

'Not really, no. Did you?'

His rage had lasted long into the night, only fuelled by the thoughts that he had misjudged her badly, and further still by the fact that he had not made love to her. He ignored her question and parried with a mock-pleasant question of his own. 'Do you have your passport with you?'

'My passport?' she echoed blankly. 'Yes, it's upstairs in my handbag.'

'Good.' He spooned Teo another mouthful and
nodded carelessly towards the dish of fruit, the basket
of fresh pastries. 'I suggest that you eat your breakfast.'

There was something so very daunting about this
icy, implacable Luis. 'I don't want any breakfast.' She
wanted to know why the hell he was asking about her
passport.

'So be it.' He shrugged. 'You will eat on the flight.'

'Flight? What flight? What are you talking about.'

'Your flight home.' He gave her a cold smile. 'I
phoned the airline first thing. There is availability on
the London flight from Madrid later on this morning.
After all, I think you will agree that there is little point
in you returning to La Rioja now.'

He was sending her away. As if she were nothing
more than an unwanted parcel! 'But what about my
things?'

'They will be forwarded on to you.'

'Just like that?'

'Just like that,' he agreed coolly.

She opened her mouth to argue with him, but the
look in his eyes told her that there was no point. He
was implacable in this. In everything. And he was
right, she *was* a fool. She had let him get close—
dangerously close—forgetting that he was offering
nothing more than his body. And then she had blown
everything—blurted out her intentions in a frustrated
state of anger and hurt, and made him think the worst.
But surely even Luis didn't really imagine that she
wanted to steal his child away?

She registered the look of censure on his face, and realised that yes, he did—and that such a crime would never go unforgiven. Or unforgotten.

The rest of the morning passed in a blur, only brought into sharp and painful focus when he announced that he would not be accompanying her to the airport.

'I am spending the morning here in the city, with my mother and Teo.'

'Oh. Oh, I see.'

'So I will say goodbye now.'

She nodded, barely able to speak, but he let her hug Teo one last time.

'Goodbye, darling,' she whispered into his dark curls, and wondered when she would ever see him again.

A car was waiting outside the hotel in the warm sunshine, ready to whisk her to the Aeropuerto de Barajas, where she boarded her plane.

Luis had booked her into first class, but Sophie might as well have been on a cattle-truck for all the notice she took of the sublime service.

And when she landed back in England, to a cold and rainy day, she felt like a foreigner in her own country.

There were tons of messages on her Ansaphone and a whole stack of mail to catch up with, and before long she rang her grandmother.

'I'm back, Granny.'

'And Teo?'

'Oh…' She had been about to say ''wait until you see him'' but she bit the words back. 'He's…lovely…just lovely. I've taken millions of photos of him for you. I'll bring them down once they've been developed.'

There was a pause. 'But you won't be bringing him?'

'Nope.'

'Luis refused, I suppose?'

'Yes, I'm afraid that he did.'

'I suspected he would,' sighed her grandmother, and Sophie heard the sadness in her voice and wondered if she should have tried to fight harder for him.

Uneasily Sophie settled back into the busy routine of work. Of running for the tube and going to noisy pubs on Fridays, and lazy Sundays spent wandering round the shops and the galleries. But she missed Teo more than she could ever have imagined—nighttimes just didn't seem the same without his splashy bath-times and bedtime story and then the sweet, baby smell of him. His little squeals of laughter when she tickled him, and his flailing, chubby arms while she taught him to swim.

The world and the life she had here in London was so different from the one she had just left behind. Almost too different. She missed the warm heat of the Spanish sun and the scent of the lemons which hung from the trees.

And she missed Luis, too. How strange was that? As if something fundamental to her life had been ripped from her, leaving her gaping, and aching— longing to hear his deep, softly-accented voice and see the enigmatic gleam of his black eyes.

So many miles away from him, it was easy to ig-nore the reason her head was trying to insist on and listen instead to the insistent clamourings of her heart.

Distance and time blurred the memory into only re-membering what it wanted to.

Something had happened along the way, and it wasn't just sexual attraction because that had always been there—though she had ruthlessly quashed it when Miranda had been alive.

But it had proved impossible to be immune to the man who had been revealed to her—a man so at odds with the husband Miranda had described.

The Luis she had observed in Spain—the caring father, the intelligent and engaging companion—could that honestly have been enough to make her fall in love with him? Because it felt like love, or, rather, it felt as painful as only unrequited love could be.

She had never experienced emotions like this before. She felt like a drowning woman trying desperately to grab hold of a slippery rock which gave her no security. As if her old world was not real any more. She was just an outsider looking in—as if the people who made up her life were merely ghostly figures flitting through it like shadows.

She sent Teo a book, and two postcards of London, and said that she hoped she would see him again, and very soon, though part of her wondered whether Luis would pass the messages on.

Please, yes, she prayed. He might mistrust her motives, but surely, despite his angry words at the time, he could not really doubt the genuine love she had for his son.

And then, one evening, just when she had almost given up hoping, she got a phone call.

She had arrived home late, after a busy but rewarding day at the office. She and Liam had spent the week pitching for the biggest deal of their lives— taking on the advertising for a car company, and in particular for the latest must-have, upmarket sports model.

And to their astonished surprise they had clinched the deal and with it a multi-million-pound contract.

There had been champagne in the local wine bar afterwards and then Liam had suggested that they all go out for supper. Sophie had declined, pleading a headache, because you couldn't really tell your work-mates that your heart was aching so much that you worried you would bring everyone's mood right down.

'You OK?' Liam had frowned.

'Of course I'm OK!' she had lied. 'I'm going to be a very rich woman!'

But what was money—what was anything, really, if you couldn't have the thing you wanted most of all?

What *had* happened to her? The cool, successful career woman had been slowly transformed into a woman who longed for the everyday pleasures of the family unit. And not just any family unit—there was a ready-made one with an unfilled vacancy of wife and mother.

Which was not on offer.

Definitely not on offer.

She picked up the phone.

'Soph-ie?'

And very nearly dropped it again.

'Luis?' she questioned breathlessly.

'Of course.' There was a pause while he relaxed,

half imagining that she might have slammed the phone down on him. And wouldn't he have deserved that? His voice softened. 'Would you like me to bring Teo over to see your grandmother?'

She closed her eyes tightly. 'Oh, Luis, really? Honestly? Do you mean it?'

'I do. Of course I do.' He sighed. Saying sorry had never come easily to him. 'Sophie, I was impetuous and blind to your own sense of duty. I should not have said to you the things I did. Once you'd gone I realised that your request was not an unreasonable one—'

'I should never have suggested I take him with me on my own.' But it would have been bizarre and inappropriate, surely, to ask Luis to accompany her back to England. As if they really *were* a couple.

'No, you shouldn't,' he agreed quietly. 'But that is done with now. Shall I come?'

'When?'

The urge to see her again consumed him. 'This weekend?'

It felt like the answer to every prayer she'd ever had. But he was just fulfilling his duty as a father, she reminded herself, not offering anything more. And even if his relationship with Alejandra was over there would be other women prepared to step into her shoes. Some beautiful Spanish woman who would make a far more suitable partner than the English cousin of his late wife.

'I'll meet you at the airport,' she promised unsteadily.

She put the phone down and rang her grandmother.

'Granny,' she said in a shaking voice, 'h-how would you like to see your grandson this weekend?'

On Saturday morning her fingers were trembling so much she could barely button up her dress, and the minutes dragged by like hours until Luis's flight touched down.

He came through the arrivals lounge, carrying Teo, his black eyes searching for her, and he felt the hot beat of desire when he saw her standing there, her blonde hair gleaming and lustrous, falling over the pale linen dress she wore.

He remembered her in his arms, the soft feel of her lips against his and the scent of her perfume bewitching him.

Sophie stood stock-still, unable to move, scarcely even able to breathe, the renewed sight of him sending her senses into overdrive. She had thought of little but him, yet the reality of his hard, lean body and proud, handsome face was a million times better than any memories.

And then Teo spotted her. 'Tho-thi!' he squealed, and she bit her trembling lip very hard as she held her arms open and the child went straight into them.

'He has missed you,' observed Luis.

Over the top of Teo's head she met the understanding dark gleam of his eyes.

'We both have,' he added softly.

It doesn't mean anything, she told herself fiercely. It doesn't.

'I've hired a car,' she managed. 'It's waiting outside. Oh, and I've bought toys and a big jigsaw for you, Teo.'

'You spoil him.'

'Why not? It's my pleasure.'

'I know it is.'

With Sophie still carrying the baby, the three of them left the airport.

'You don't own a car?' questioned Luis, once he had strapped Teo into the baby-seat.

She shook her head. 'There's no need to, really, not in London. I can walk, or get the tube—or taxis if it's raining.'

'And it is always raining?' He smiled.

'Certainly more than in La Rioja,' she agreed gravely.

Her grandmother was waiting by the door when the car drew up and the old-fashioned cottage garden looked just the same as it had done when Sophie had been a little girl. Hollyhocks and roses and clematis scrambled in profusion over the stone walls of the house.

'Hello, Luis,' smiled Mrs Mills, and then she looked long and hard at the black-haired child, her lined face lighting up in delight. 'And you must be Teo.'

It was warm enough to eat lunch in the garden, and Teo sat playing happily on a blanket on the lawn with his brand-new multi-activity centre, which made all different kinds of noises.

And afterwards he began to yawn, and they drank their coffee inside while he snuggled down happily on the sofa and eventually fell asleep.

Now what? thought Sophie, but to her surprise Luis and her grandmother began chatting together quite happily. She doesn't hate him at all, Sophie realised as she began to stack the plates and carry them through to the kitchen.

She loaded everything into the dishwasher, and when she came back her grandmother looked up.

'Why don't you take the opportunity to show Luis around the village?' she suggested. 'Teo is out for the count.'

Sophie looked at Luis. 'Do you want to?'

'Sure, why not?' he agreed evenly. 'You know for yourself that he will sleep one, maybe two hours.'

They walked down the lane, past the church. 'They have the most beautiful bell-ringing in there,' she said, though her breath was coming erratically. 'And up here is the post office. We were always allowed an ice lolly if we were—'

'Sophie,' he said suddenly, 'Salvadora is moving away.'

'Moving?' She stopped in her tracks. 'Moving where?'

'Back to Salamanca, where her family live. Pirro, too. She is getting old—far too old to care for Teo now. I realised that once you had gone. And she is happy to leave—the child is too much for her, I real- ised that, too, and I saw for myself the difference in the way you had been with Teo. Young enough to play with him as he should be played with.'

Her brows criss-crossed in confusion. How on earth would he be able to cope without Salvadora? 'What will you do? Who is going to look after him from now on?'

'I will have to advertise for someone.' He watched carefully for her reaction. 'Someone young.' A pause. 'Someone like you.'

She met his eyes, her heart leaping in her chest as she dared to ask the question without questioning the folly of doing so. 'But not me?'

He paused. 'You have your life here,' he said deliberately.

Did she? What kind of life was it now? A life she would willingly swap to be with the man she ached for. But he wasn't asking her to be with him.

'You mean you don't want me,' she said painfully, the wrench in her heart sending the words spilling out of her mouth of their own accord.

His mouth lost some of its habitual tightness as he relaxed. 'Oh, Sophie,' he drawled, pulling her into his arms without warning, his black eyes blazing with ebony fire as he stared down into her face. 'That is just the trouble, *querida*. I do want you. Believe me, I want you in every way that a man wants a woman.'

'Luis…' But she didn't move. Couldn't. In his arms was the place she most wanted to be.

'I want to make love to you, Sophie.' His rich voice caressed her like the fingertips which were tracing tiny paths over the peachy bloom of her cheeks. 'You have set me on fire,' he whispered. 'A fire which burns in my veins, filling me with thoughts of you and desire for you, a desire which can no longer be denied, no matter how hard I try. And yes, I want you to come back to La Rioja and to care for Teo as you have already done so beautifully, but most of all— God, forgive me—I want you in my bed.'

And she wanted to be there, more than anything else in the world, but… 'But what about Miranda?' she whispered, and guilt was as strong as it had ever been. 'What would she say?'

'Miranda is dead,' he said, a note of sadness making his voice soft, and quiet. 'And we are living. Do you not think she would want us to be happy?'

Happy? It was an interesting choice of word. Was he guaranteeing her happiness, or merely the see-sawing of violent emotions and passion which would bring her no lasting peace?

She sighed. 'I don't know.'

'Deny yourself this and you will regret it for the rest of your days,' he breathed. 'I know how much you want me, Sophie. I can read it in your eyes and on your lips. And your body tells me in no uncertain tones that your desire matches mine. Tell me that is not true.' His black eyes bored into her. 'No,' he finished on a small note of triumph. 'You cannot.'

No, she could not, but there was more at stake here than mere desire. Her life. Her career—and, most importantly of all, her fragile heart. She raised her face to his, staring with concentration into his eyes. 'It isn't that simple, Luis.'

'It's as simple as you make it,' he contradicted softly. 'And this easy.'

His mouth came down to meet hers and her gasp of protest was stifled by the sheer pleasure of his kiss. She heedlessly tried to tell herself that this was sheer madness. That he was offering her nothing more than his body and his companionship, while she, as a woman, wanted so much more from him than that. But her reasoning dissolved into nothing as his mouth explored hers. 'Luis,' she said brokenly against his mouth and opened her lips to his.

That first intimate contact of the flesh awoke an explosion of need in him so powerful that he could have pinned her to the ground, loosened her clothing and thrust himself into her sweet, ripe flesh right there and then. He felt the warm, moist cavern of her mouth, the flicker of her tongue against his, and he grew painfully hard in an instant, wanting to spill his seed and go on and on spilling his seed.

They each broke the kiss at the same instant, though for entirely different reasons.

Sophie ran her hand distractedly through her ruffled blonde hair. 'You're asking an awful lot of me, Luis.'

'I know I am.'

To give up everything she had here, in her safe, comfortable and predictable life in England—with nothing offered in return other than his body and his son and to live with him in the beautiful hacienda which nestled in the valleys of La Rioja. No declaration of love—but he has never been a hypocrite, she reminded herself. Nor a long-standing promise of commitment.

He was offering her more than he had offered Alejandra, it was true, but was she allowing herself to forget how conveniently he had discarded her? Wouldn't only a desperate fool grab at an opportunity like this?

But then she thought of the alternative—of the grey reality of life without the charismatic, vital Spaniard, and she knew then that sometimes in life you had to take risks. Emotional risks.

Sure, she had taken risks when she had started up the fledgling company with Liam, but that had been different—financial. She'd had a lot less to lose.

She thought about it some more.

She was twenty-seven years old and he had spoken

nothing but the truth when he had said that if she denied herself this then she would regret it for the rest of her days. And if it did go wrong, she could rebuild her life in London again. She could even start another advertising agency. She'd done it once, so she could do it again. But this might be her only chance with Luis.

What if she ended up bitter and unfulfilled—a woman who asked herself the heartbreakingly unanswerable question of what would have happened 'if only'?

Did he guess at her momentary weakness; was that why he moved in for the kill with his velvet-voiced question, like a matador moving in to claim the stunned bull for his own?

'Will you, Sophie, will you come and live with me in La Rioja?'

There was a heartbeat of a pause while she considered the alternative. 'I will,' she said in a low voice, thinking with a kind of poignant longing how much like a wedding vow that sounded. But he was not offering her marriage. He had been honest to a fault. He wanted her, yes, and he was entrusting her with the care of his son. But not love. Not marriage. His mistress and his son's carer.

It was not enough and yet, in a mad and inexplicable way, it was more than enough. Certainly more than she had here, without her proud, arrogant Spaniard who dominated her thoughts as no other man had done.

Nor would again, she recognised painfully. He was right. If she lived to be a hundred no sweet, tantalising opportunity like this would come her way again. She must seize it. Live it and relish it, day by day and night by night. She would give it a year—if it lasted that long—and then she would rethink her future. 'I will,' she said again.

But he needed to be sure. 'You would leave all this behind?'

'I would.'

'Why?'

'Because of T-Teo,' she faltered, and saw his face suddenly become shuttered, the eyes narrowing as he nodded almost imperceptibly.

'Sì. Por Teo.'

Something had made his voice colourless, and she sought to put the passion back. 'And...and for you, Luis.'

'But what for me, exactly, *querida?*' he questioned softly.

'I want you,' she admitted simply, struggling to elaborate in a way which would not terrify him into retracting his offer.

For wouldn't a man like Luis run a mile if he suspected that her heart was already lost to him?

'I want to sh-share your bed. I want you to make love to me,' she said shakily, because in this, at least, she would be as honest as it was in her power to be. She lifted her fingers and touched them to his black hair. 'I want what you can give me, Luis. What a man can give a woman.'

But not any man. Only this man.

He stared down at her, seeing the fleeting look of vulnerability in her blue eyes, unable to give her the reassurance he knew she needed and deserved. Maybe he *did* have no heart—but surely it would be unfair to express an emotion he did not feel?

He told himself that he had been through a lot lately—and that Sophie herself came with all the baggage of being Miranda's cousin.

He wanted her, yes—more than he could remember wanting any woman—but was what he felt for her nothing more than dressed-up lust? And wouldn't it be unforgivable if he could offer her nothing more than that?

But then her lips parted in silent invitation, and he was lost. Lost.

He gave a small groan as he lifted his hand and caught hers, drawing it close to his lips and slowly kissing each fingertip while his eyes captured hers in their ebony glitter.

'And can you just walk out on your company without a backward glance?'

'I'll have to think about that.' Maybe she could work part-time from Spain in some kind of executive capacity. Or would it be kinder to Liam and the company to sever her ties with it completely? Would the release of her equity free her from worry—the interest from her capital allowing her to continue to be independent? For she would not, she realised fiercely, be a kept woman. Not under any circumstances. She smiled up into his frowning eyes, and shrugged. 'As I've said before, Luis—no one is indispensable.'

But she had come pretty close to being indispensable to Teo, he recognised, not for the first time. She loved him and cared for him in a way that Miranda had not been able to do, God rest her soul.

'Do you know, I would like to take you somewhere

now and to seal this agreement with my lips and my body?' he said thickly. 'Shall we do that, Sophie? Is there somewhere…private…for us?'

Seal this agreement. How coldly he expressed himself! But even the pragmatic words could not dampen her hunger for him, and for one insane moment she considered taking him further up the lane, to where her childhood hideaway lay hidden within the wooded copse, where they would not be disturbed…

'And I would like that more than anything else,' she whispered, trying not to conjure up an erotic vision of him making love to her outdoors, right now. And then imagined what a sight they would make, returning to the house, covered in twigs and little bits of grass, their faces flushed and their eyes hectic! 'But we can't,' she groaned. 'My grandmother is waiting. And Teo, too. We have responsibilities, Luis.'

How ironic that what he admired in her he also resented! But she was right—they *did* have responsibilities.

'*Sì.*' His body ached as much as he suspected hers did, and yet he admired her cool restraint, the step back she had now taken to distance herself. Keeping him waiting and waiting, and wanting even more… 'Then let us go,' he agreed unsteadily. 'For unless we have a chaperon I will have to kiss you into submission, *querida.*'

'What makes you think you would be able to?' she teased.

'Shall we put it to the test?' he challenged provocatively, and moved closer, his dark, haunting features mocking her with their beauty.

But she shook her head, not trusting her own resolve in the face of such an offer. She tried and failed to imagine any other man getting away with such a masterful and silken boast, and shivered, wondering if she had taken on more than she could ever have anticipated with Luis de la Camara.

'You'll have us arrested,' she said, only half joking.

CHAPTER NINE

'So YOU are here at last,' Luis breathed. 'At long last.'

Sophie's mouth dried as she gazed back at him, dressed in a billowy shirt of snowy-white and fitted jet trousers which made him look as though he should be bull-running in the nearby city of Pamplona.

'Y-yes,' she agreed shakily. 'Here at last.'

Once more he had met her at the airport, and they had just endured a car journey of almost unendurable tension. She had badly wanted him to kiss her, but he had not, and now that Teo had been put to bed he seemed reluctant still, and she did not know why, nor dared to ask.

Surely he was not now regretting his decision to ask her here, not after she had spent the last month tidying up her life back in England to accommodate an arrangement which was seeming increasingly bizarre by the second. Why did he stand so far from her, such an intimidating and untouching distance away from her?

He savoured the moment—the anticipation and the expectation—for just a little while longer. His hunger was unbearable, aroused to such a pitch by the fact that something denied to him so long was finally to be his.

He had not dared touch her at the airport, nor in the car, and not simply because this time he had brought Teo and his presence was inhibiting, but because Luis feared that once he touched her he would explode. And it was no fitting way to begin if he pulled over on some deserted stretch of the highway and made love to her in the cramped conditions of the car, with his small son in the back.

No, it would not be fitting.

He wanted a bed—and once he had her in it he feared that he would never be able to get out of it again.

He poured her a glass of wine and handed it to her. 'So, was it easy to leave?'

She took the wine, grateful and yet slightly resentful. He sounded as though he was interviewing her for a job—which in a way, she reminded herself painfully, he was.

'Not what I'd call easy,' she admitted, and sipped the de la Camara Rioja.

'Oh?' He raised his dark brows in imperious question.

She would not admit that almost everyone had tried to talk her out of it. Her parents had asked her worriedly if she knew what she was doing. Liam had told her frankly that she was 'mad.' And her grandmother had looked positively worried.

'Oh, Sophie, are you *sure?*'

'I love Teo,' said Sophie doggedly.

'Just Teo?' Mrs Mills queried perceptively.

'What do you mean?'

'Just what exactly is your role going to be? As sole carer for Teo?'

'Not sole carer, no, of course not. Luis will be hands-on whenever he isn't working. And there's a girl from the village who can babysit, apparently. Oh, and a new cook and gardener, and a housekeeper,' she added almost vaguely, and saw her grandmother raise her eyebrows fractionally.

'And that's all?'

Sophie sighed, not knowing whether to tell her grandmother the truth or not—but how could you possibly tell a woman of nearly eighty that you had agreed to become the mistress of a man you had always affected to despise?

'It's hard to explain,' she said falteringly. 'I don't know what's going to happen—'

'You're in love with him, aren't you?'

Sophie bit her lip, unwilling to lie, but even more unwilling to cause her grandmother disquiet. And besides, who could say? She thought that yes, she *was* in love with him, but maybe love was a word women used when they wanted to dress up the fact that they desired a man with a ferocity which left them slightly dazed?

'I don't know what I really feel.' She turned her eyes beseechingly towards her grandmother. 'I know that you think he did Miranda wrong, and that he's all bad—'

'I never said that,' interrupted her grandmother firmly. 'No one person is all bad, and no one person is all good, either—but two people may not be good for each other, and I think that was the case for Miranda and Luis.' She rubbed at the knuckles of her fingers. 'Just be careful, dear, that's all I'm saying. I can see the obvious attraction in a man like Luis, but he may not be good for you either.'

Sophie had remembered her words on the flight

over, recognising that her grandmother was probably speaking a truth she did not really wish to hear, but recognising also that she was in too deep now to back off. She had committed herself to Teo, and she had committed herself to his father, except that his father now stood like some gorgeous but unapproachable stranger on the other side of the high-ceilinged sitting room of the hacienda.

Well, she was damned if she was going to make the first move. Hadn't she given up enough to be here—did he want total capitulation into the bargain?

Luis could see the tension which had stiffened her shoulders. She looked uptight and brittle—as if she was regretting her decision to come. But she was bound to have doubts, and if he leapt on her with all the finesse of a teenager then might she not feel used, as women sometimes did?

'Sit down.' He gave a glimmer of a smile.

This was worse than unendurable. Was this what she had left her life in England for? This brittle expectation? The air was tight with the tension of knowing precisely why she was here—that they were going to make love at last, after a wait which seemed to have gone on for a lifetime. He knew it and she knew it, and suddenly she felt a little like a commodity.

She put her glass down with a shaky bang. 'I don't want to sit down. I think I might go upstairs to freshen up. I'm—I'm tired.'

But the thought of her disappearing was unendurable. *Madre de Dios!* He had tried to play the perfect host and gentleman, and not the would-be lover whose groin was on fire with need—but it seemed that Sophie Mills wanted none of these.

He put his own glass down and moved towards her with the stealth and grace of a panther. 'You want to go upstairs, *querida?*' he questioned silkily.

She studied her shoes. 'That's what I said.'

'And which room were you planning to use?'

'The room I had before.' Of that she had been sure. Mistresses kept some kind of distance, didn't they? And keeping her distance might be the only way she could put some kind of barrier around her vulnerable heart.

'No, you move into mine,' he negated implacably. 'You sleep with me. Only with me. Sophie.'

She looked up into his face, some honeyed quality of his words making it impossible not to. 'Luis?' she whispered.

'I have waited for too long now.' He kissed her then, because nothing in the world could have kept him back any longer.

And she too had waited for more than long enough. Was that his intention—to hold her at arm's length until she would be so filled with need for him that she would become a melting, responsive mass in his arms?

Because that was exactly what happened.

'L—' She tried to say his name, but his mouth blotted the word out and she clung to him as he enfolded her, smoothing his hands down over her hair, and then moving them down to cup her breasts, making a small groan against her lips as he did so.

'Oh, God!' She swayed against him, feeling her nipples peak against his palms in a blatant signal of need, feeling his hand now moving to the slight curve of her belly, brushing carelessly down over her dress and alighting very deliberately over where she was beginning to ache very badly indeed.

She squirmed against him as he deepened the kiss until she could barely think. Her body was on fire and she seemed to be all glorious and aching sensation, when, abruptly, he stopped and she stared up at him in silent reprimand, seeing the hectic, inky glitter of his eyes and the soft wash of colour which accentuated his aristocratic cheekbones.

'You want me to take you here, on the floor, *querida?*' he questioned in a voice made husky with desire. 'Is that your intention?'

Her breath coming in short little bursts, she stared back at him. Why fight her needs, or her desires? She was here on his terms, yes—but also on her own. And, as a mistress, then surely she had the right to tell him exactly what she wanted…?

'Or on the sofa, perhaps?' she suggested.

His pulses leapt even more at her erotic suggestion, and he growled and caught her against him again, wondering if she was like this with all her lovers.

'The first time should be in bed,' he ground out, and simply picked her up and carried her out of the room.

This was ridiculous—like a crazy fantasy come true. No man had ever stridden with her held so effortlessly and so masterfully in his arms, and Sophie felt almost faint with pleasure.

'I think you've been watching too many old movies,' she joked weakly.

'I think not,' came the unequivocal reply, and as he mounted the stairs he bent his head to her breast, suckling her through the cotton dress she wore, and

Sophie scrabbled her fingernails in frantic pleasure against his back.

'Stop it!' she murmured.

He didn't move, just gave one deliberate lick of his tongue and felt her shudder in response. 'Why? Don't you like it?'

Her head fell back. 'Y-yes,' she gasped.

But her answer was redundant. As he lifted his head to look at her he could see that she liked it very much.

As did he. With a groan he opened the door to his bedroom, and softly kicked it shut before carrying her straight over to the bed and placing her down on it, standing with his hands on his hips while he steadied his breathing.

Madre de Dios, but she looked beautiful! Almost wanton, with her flushed cheeks and her honey hair spilling in disarray, even though the dress she wore was decent enough.

Too decent.

He sat down on the edge of the bed and began to unbutton it, and Sophie watched him, mesmerised, as he freed her from the constricting garment. The cool air washed over her skin as he peeled away the still damp fabric from her breasts.

He sucked in a breath as he slid the dress from over her shoulders, the sight of her in her underwear making his heart rate undergo a dramatic change.

He had seen her in a swimsuit, of course, but a swimsuit, no matter how revealing, was very different from a bra and some flimsy little panties.

He ran a questing finger thoughtfully over a breast

covered with apricot lace and trimmed with tiny rose buds.

'These are new?'

To her horror, Sophie found herself blushing as she nodded and nerves suddenly assailed her again. 'Yes.' Did it seem like the world's biggest cliché, then, to come to him in brand-new underwear? Wasn't it all just a little too obvious?

'You pay me a great compliment, *querida,*' he murmured, then narrowed his eyes as he saw her swift rise in colour. She seemed almost…almost… Surely she was not *nervous?* 'Do I frighten you, little one?' he asked, almost reflectively.

Frighten her? No, *he* didn't frighten her—but for some reason she felt utterly petrified. Shouldn't he have tried out the goods first? she thought, verging on the brink of hysteria. What if she disappointed him in bed; what price his mistress then?

But now he had gently begun to stroke her belly, and despite her misgivings, Sophie began to relax, all her reservations gradually dissolving into nothing as he incited a slow build-up of pleasure to replace them.

She let her eyes drift to a close, and sighed.

Luis watched her. She puzzled and perplexed him. One moment she was writhing passionately in his arms, while the next, staring up at him almost nervously, as if she was a virgin—and he was prepared to bet his entire fortune that she was not.

'Unbutton my shirt, *querida,*' he urged softly, and dipped his finger into her belly button in an erotic mimicry of the ultimate possession.

Sophie opened her eyes and looked at him sitting beside her, so dark and so beautiful. She let her gaze wander to where he still stroked her belly, his fingertips tracing such erotic pathways over its slight swell. Eagerly she lifted her hands up and freed the first button of his shirt, then the next, scarcely able to resist a gasp as his torso was made bare for her delight.

His skin was bronze and roughened with dark hair, and his stomach was flat and hard. She freed the final button and he shrugged it off with an arrogant gesture of dismissal, staring down at her with a look of unashamed hunger and a fierce kind of tension.

And his hunger matched her own and gave her strength. Courage. Confidence to play the role he would expect. His lover, his *equal*.

She teased her fingertips over the buckle of his belt and then withdrew them, glancing up at him from between half-slitted lashes. 'Shall I?'

But he had anticipated her question before she uttered it and he caught hold of her hand, transferring it to where he felt he might explode with hardness and then deliberately moving it away again. 'No,' he whispered.

'No?' She stared at him in confusion. Maybe he only liked passive women—women who would lie back and do nothing?

He shook his head and stood up. He felt so aroused—unbearably aroused—and he was afraid that she might injure him, however dexterous she was. '*Querida.*' He gave a rueful smile. 'I will have enough difficulty taking the damned things off myself!'

Some of the tension left her and she watched him, enjoying the show as his body was gradually revealed.

Wincing slightly, he unzipped the black trousers and stepped out of them, roughly pulling off the dark socks and silk boxer shorts until he was left in nothing at all, and Sophie thought that she had never seen a man more magnificent, nor more at ease with his nakedness.

He came to her and lay down beside her, smoothing her hair back as he took her in his arms. He unclasped her bra, letting out a little cry of delight as her breasts fell free and unfettered against him.

'At last,' he breathed, and dipped his head to their lush swell, burying his face in their swollen splendour. '*Madre de Dios*—at last!'

He took one rosy nub into his mouth and licked it and teased it with his teeth, a sensation so exquisite that Sophie cried out with the pleasure of it, clutching at his shoulders in helpless surrender.

'Luis,' she whispered. 'Oh, Luis.'

'I know, *querida*,' he said in an unfamiliar shaky voice. 'I know.'

He could feel her slender curves contrasted against the angular planes of his own body and the rough brush of lace against the hard cradle of him seemed too much of a barrier. He lifted his head from breast to mouth and his hand drifted downwards, hooking into the delicate fabric at her hips. 'These I no longer wish to see, or to feel,' he husked, bringing his lips down to hers, and sliding off the tiny lace panties.

Sophie shivered uncontrollably, unable to keep her body still as he tracked his hand down her thigh.

But he shushed her. '*Querida*, don't move,' he said, with a slight note of desperation in his voice. 'You are driving me crazy.'

She tried, but it was hard not to squirm with excitement as he manoeuvred the delicate wisp down until it lay forgotten, coiled like the tail of a kitten around one ankle. Luxuriously, she touched his back, kneading her fingers possessively against the silken skin, and then moving them round to trickle through the thick whorls of hair at his chest, feeling him shudder in response when she feather-lighted her way over each tiny nipple.

He closed his eyes briefly, begging his body for control, then tipped her head back and looked down at her, his black eyes glittering sternly, though his lips held the trace of a smile. 'You test my patience, Sophie,' he said unsteadily.

'I don't want to test anything,' she whispered.

For answer, he slipped his hand between her thighs and smiled as her mouth opened in startled pleasure.

Sophie's eyes widened as he began to touch her. 'Luis,' she swallowed. 'Luis, please…'

He felt as if he might explode when he found her wet, wild heat, felt her move her hips in instant response. His erection pushed insistently against his stomach. Had he ever felt so hard before? 'What is it?' he beseeched her. 'Tell me what it is you want?'

It was difficult to get the words out when he was touching her intimately like that, his face so close to hers, so that she was unable to hide from him what she wanted most of all. 'You,' she choked. 'Now. Please.'

Their eyes met in a moment of complete understanding.

Her fears were gone, he recognised, but those fears might build again if he played with her. He wanted to tease her and take her to the very brink, so that her pleasure would be all the more intense, but he recognised that enough was enough.

She needed no games, nor demonstrations of his finesse. She was ready for him and all she needed was him—deep, deep inside her.

With a groan he moved away and reached to his locker, so that in a moment all he was wearing was a condom.

Sophie quickly closed her eyes in case he saw her reaction as he slid it on, for Luis needed no boost to his already well-developed ego. She swallowed, thinking that his ego wasn't the only part of him which was well-developed.

Oh, perfect man, she thought, almost despairingly. How could any other compete with Luis de la Camara?

But then he was back beside her, kissing her until she thought that she might faint with pleasure. He murmured to her in Spanish—hauntingly soft and huskily evocative phrases which made her even wilder for him. And that was when he moved on top of her.

She had longed and prayed for just this, and now that the moment was here she felt physically excited yet emotionally…well, emotionally she was as mixed-up as she had ever been. But why allow her insecurity to get in the way of such long-awaited pleasure? What purpose would it serve other than for one to cancel out the other?

His hardness was daunting—beautifully daunting— pushing teasingly against her, and, though part of her wanted to prolong the delicious anticipation, she couldn't. Please, she begged him silently. Please.

Did he read her mind, or was the waiting just too much for him as well? For suddenly he thrust into her, filling her with warmth and with himself, and her eyes flew open to find him looking down at her, his face tight with tension, as if he was reining himself in only with the most monumental effort.

He bent his head and kissed her, blotting out everything other than sensation as he began to move inside her, and Sophie had never felt so alive before, so at one, their bodies meeting and joining and moving in perfect synchrony, as if they had been designed only for each other.

So that when she felt the beckoning of pleasure she gave a little cry of disbelief and disappointment, for it was too soon and she didn't want it to end.

He stopped kissing her and stared down, his eyes completely black. 'What is it, *querida?*' he questioned unsteadily, but he didn't stop moving, and because of that it was too late, and she…she…

'Luis!' His name was torn from her lips as the delicious spasms caught her up in their indefinable dance.

Still thrusting into her, he gazed down at her enraptured face, wanting to watch her and enjoy her pleasure, but it was not to be. For just as she arched her back and flung her head back, just as her legs stiffened and the slow flush of orgasm bloomed like a flower on her pale skin, he felt his own release coming.

She fluttered her eyelids open and saw the tension

leave the dark, sculpted face, heard him groan as he drove himself into her over and over and over again.

Only when he was spent, and had dropped a kiss onto the tip of her nose, and yawned, and withdrawn, did Sophie wonder what on earth they did now.

Imperceptibly she shifted away from the dark olive body. 'Shall I—shall I sleep here tonight?' she asked.

He frowned. Was this her idea of a joke? One trip to heaven and back was enough for her? Granting him the ultimate intimacy whilst denying him the pleasure of holding her in his arms during the night?

He lay back and stared at the whirling fan above his head. 'If you wish to.'

He sounded as if he didn't care one way or the other. Maybe in the circumstances a little protective space might be just what they needed. Or what *she* needed. 'I could go next door,' she suggested. 'You'd get more sleep that way.'

She pushed the sheet aside, revealing her long, pale limbs as she began to swing them over the side of the bed, and in that instant Luis knew that he was not letting her go anywhere. And he would pleasure her so much that she would never make such an outrageous proposal again.

'But I have no wish to sleep, Sophie,' he said, pulling her back towards him, his fingers idly beginning to stroke at her breast.

The sensation was bewitching, but she wondered what had put that odd kind of note in his voice. If she asked him what he was really feeling right now, would he tell her?

But that was when he cupped her breast and took

it between his lips once more, and Sophie turned with a little moan, forgetting the questions in her mind and giving herself up to the renewed demands of her body instead.

CHAPTER TEN

SOPHIE moved across the sunlit garden towards the swimming pool to the sound of echoing laughter, and as she made her way through the shaded canopy of the trees and saw Luis rubbing suncream into Teo's back her breath caught in her throat, just the way it always did. She sighed.

She had thought it impossible that her feelings for him should grow even stronger, but in that she had been proved completely wrong.

Three months of living with him as his mistress had done nothing to diminish the earth-shattering effect he had on her. Though maybe that wasn't surprising. Didn't making love night after night with a man only heighten your emotions when you were in love with him?

If only…she thought wistfully…if only he loved her back. But he didn't and he wouldn't and she would just have to learn to live with it. And she couldn't really complain—because he treated her with all the true, innate courtesy she would have expected from his aristocratic upbringing.

He laughed at her jokes and she laughed at his. They read the newspapers over breakfast and discussed world affairs just as if they were a real couple. Sometimes he taught her words and phrases in Spanish, so that she might gradually learn to speak his native tongue.

So what was missing? Words of undying love and devotion? She had known from the beginning what the score was, and if she expected those then she was doomed to be disappointed. He wasn't breaking any promises to her, because he had not made any.

Luis lifted his head and saw her, his black eyes narrowing as he observed the striking vision she made, before a slow smile lit up the hard, proud features. *'Buenos dias, Sophie,'* he murmured, his soft voice carrying across the still air.

He was just too devastatingly good-looking, she thought as she grew closer, and not for the first time it seemed to her unfair that one man should have been given quite so many attributes.

Tiny beads of water glistened like diamonds on the burnished muscles. His skin was an even deeper olive colour now, tanned lightly by the sun, as smooth and luxurious as oiled silk, broken only by the dark hair which spattered his chest, arrowing down in an enticing line towards the black trunks.

Not skimpy trunks, like those worn by so many men on beach holidays, but in a way these were even more provocative. They hugged the curve of his buttocks and caressed the hard shaft of his thighs. The body she knew so well, the body she could never have enough of.

Composing her face so that it was free of any giveaway yearning, she smiled.

'Tho-thi!' squealed Teo in delight as he caught sight of her.

Sophie sped up and ran the last short distance towards him with her arms outstretched, as delighted now as she had been the first time he had managed his own distinctive version of her name!

'Buenos dias, Teodoro!' she beamed. *'Como estas?'*

As usual, her attempt at Spanish made him giggle uncontrollably and she ruffled his hair affectionately. 'You wait!' she teased, waggling a finger at him. 'Soon my Spanish will be better than yours!'

Luis sucked in a breath as she crouched down beside him, the fall of honey-coloured hair resolutely hiding her expression as he silently cursed and applauded her for her choice of swimsuit. He had never known a woman so modest!

Not for her the minuscule combination of three tiny triangles linked together with nothing more than a wisp of string. In his experience, most women used swimming as an opportunity to show off as much of their bodies as possible, but not Sophie.

Yet the blue of her suit enhanced her eyes, its high cut emphasising the long, long legs—and, although most of her breasts were concealed, the thin fabric did nothing to disguise their sinful curve. Breasts which pillowed his head at night when he slept…

'Vamos a nadar?' asked Sophie tentatively as she flapped her arms around in a swimming gesture.

'Sì, sì!' giggled Teodoro and held his arms up to her.

Sophie picked him up, breathing in the gorgeous baby scent of him as he wrapped his little sun creamed arms trustingly around her neck, yet she was aware of the black eyes following her every movement.

'Are you coming in?' she asked.

Luis frowned, distracted. 'Mmm?'

'Swimming?'

He shook his head, not trusting himself to move, he was so aroused. 'I'll stay here and watch.'

But sitting on the sidelines and observing her un-inhibited splashing around with his son did little for his equilibrium. He stifled a groan and turned onto his stomach.

He had always longed for a woman who did not make impossible emotional demands on him, but now that he had found one he discovered that he was be-coming increasingly frustrated.

Just what was it about Sophie? She never sought compliments, nor tried to engineer bouts of jealousy by flirting with his friends on the occasions when they had gone out to dinner as a couple. Nor did she de-mand to know how he 'felt' about her.

She adored Teo and never seemed to get irritated at the increasing demands he made on her. She was both cool and passionate, analytical and clever—ev-erything a man could wish for.

So what was the matter with him?

'You looked miles away.'

A soft voice broke into his reverie and he looked up to see Sophie standing with water streaming in rivulets down her body, reaching down to pick up a towel to dry the wet toddler in her arms.

And treating him to a heart-stoppingly clear view of her cleavage, he thought savagely, wishing that they had a babysitter right now, so that he could take her off to bed and...

'Luis, what *is* the matter?'

'Why should anything be the matter?' he demanded shortly.

'I don't know. You were scowling, that's all.'

He closed his eyes. 'I'm just tired.'

No wonder, she thought lovingly as she watched the slow rise and fall of his back. By rights, she should have felt tired, too, seeing as how they had barely snatched any sleep last night. A smile curved the edges of her mouth as she dabbed at Teo's curls. The amazing thing was that she didn't feel tired in the least—she felt as if she could go out and run a marathon!

Later that evening, at dinner, he stared at her through the flickering light of the candles. 'Do you want to go to a party?'

Sophie blinked. 'When?'

'Tomorrow night.'

'That's a bit short notice, isn't it?'

'I was…undecided,' he said slowly. 'But I think you might enjoy it.'

He seemed in an odd mood tonight, she thought. Distracted. Tense. The black eyes looking even more enigmatic than usual.

But a party might be fun. 'OK, that sounds good,' she smiled. 'Shall I ring for dessert now?'

He felt infuriatingly disappointed at her lack of questioning. Why wasn't she quizzing him about where the party was and who was throwing it, and who would be there? Almost, he thought with another frown, as if she couldn't care less.

In truth, Sophie was nervous inside, but she was damned if she was going to let Luis know. She found the wives and partners of his friends unbelievably gorgeous and impeccably groomed. Most of them looked as though they had spent an exhausting day going from gym, to manicurist, pedicurist, hairdresser and then home, for some intensive work in getting ready to go out.

Not that she was a slouch in the dressing-up department, but she just felt on the wrong side of sophisticated in comparison. For a start, her nails were short and unvarnished—mainly because she seemed to spend a good deal of her day sitting beneath the shade of the lemon trees and playing in the sandpit with Teo, and sand tended to play havoc with anything approaching talons!

The following evening she opened the door to her wardrobe and surveyed the contents. No shortage of smart new clothes for her smart new life.

Selling her share of the business had left her a wealthy woman—well, only very relatively rich when compared with Luis, she supposed wryly.

Luis had taken her shopping in Pamplona for clothes suited to the hot La Rioja summer and once again she had thwarted his attempts to pay for her purchases.

'I can pay myself,' she had said stubbornly. 'I've sold the business, remember?'

'*Madre de Dios!*' he had exclaimed. 'You are a stubborn woman! You know that it is quite different now!'

'How?'

'You look after my son,' he had asserted. 'For which I would have to pay anyone else!'

'Maybe some day I'll ask you to,' she had said

serenely. 'At the moment I don't need it. And besides, I'm doing it for love, not money.'

He had opened his mouth and shut it again, unable to argue with her logic, and she had seen both frustration and admiration sparking from his eyes. Good! For she had long since decided that Luis de la Camara had stereotyped women for far too long now. Let him realise that there were many variations of a woman and they weren't all out for what they could get!

She took from the wardrobe a dress which she had not yet worn—a filmy, floaty scrap of pink with spaghetti straps which made the most of her light tan, and a just-above-the-knee skirt which made the most of her long legs.

Just as she had done for the wedding, she wore more make-up than usual, not just for the effect, but because make-up sometimes provided a mask you could hide behind. And she was well-aware of the eyes which would be watching her, the eyes which longed to ask just what was really happening between her and the Don, but didn't dare.

Luis was waiting downstairs for her and when she walked into the room he wondered why in God's name he had agreed to go to the damned party after all. They could have stayed here. Eaten finer food and drunk infinitely finer wines. He could have slowly undressed her and made love to her here, and then taken her upstairs and carried on...

A pulse beat insistently in his cheek. 'You look very beautiful, *querida*,' he murmured, and beckoned her. 'Come here.'

His eyes compelled her, as did the sultry note of command in his voice. But the hectic glitter in his black eyes warned her that it would be dangerous to do as he suggested, especially when—she took a quick glance at her watch—when they were due at a party.

'Luis—'

'Come here,' he repeated, and a small smile lifted the corners of his hard mouth as she came and stood before him.

'Luis—' she protested weakly as he lowered his head to kiss the skin of her bare shoulder, sending little shivers of sensation tingling over her body.

'Come and sit down,' he purred, and led her over to the sofa.

'But I thought we were going to the party—'

'We are.' He kissed her neck again and felt her shudder as he drifted his hand over her breast. 'In a minute.' His fingers began to trace feather-light paths over her nipples. 'Do you remember the night you arrived, and suggested making love on the sofa?'

'Stop it—'

'You don't want me to?'

No, she didn't, but if *someone* didn't put a stop to it then she knew exactly what was going to happen. And her heart started thundering against her breast as her body began to greedily anticipate just what that was.

'Stop it,' she whispered again, but this time her voice was slurred with a deepening note of desire.

'No, let's start it.' He took her hand and travelled it to where he was so hard that he knew he would be unable to set foot outside this house unless he rid himself of the unbelievable ache.

Her legs felt weak and her hands were shaking but

somehow she unzipped him, her fingers faltering as she felt the enormous power of him springing free, and she saw from the tightening tension on his face that he was close to losing control.

With a slow, sultry smile she took control, pushing him down on the sofa and edging his trousers down, before deftly stepping out of her panties and dropping them carelessly to the floor.

'*Querida!*' he gasped, and then gasped again as she sat astride him, taking him deep inside her and wrapping her arms tightly around him as she began to move.

It was all over very quickly, too quickly, he thought with a pang of regret as he waited for her fluttering little spasms to subside.

Eventually he lifted her from him, a rueful smile touching his lips.

'Come, *querida,* or we're going to be late for our party.'

She wondered what she must look like—flushed and warm and sticky and replete. 'You still want to go?' she asked uncertainly.

His mouth hardened as he forced himself to remember that what had just happened had been nothing more than a sweet diversion. 'Yes.'

She swallowed. 'Give me five minutes.'

She took ten, but when she reappeared, with her hair brushed and smelling of soap and scent—sexy, yet demure—it was hard to believe what a little wildcat she had just been. He held her pashmina out for her. 'Let's go,' he said shortly.

Sophie sat in the car, muddled and confused. Sex was supposed to bring you closer, wasn't it? So why did Luis suddenly seem like a million miles away from her?

She struggled to lighten the inexplicable tension which had descended on them.

'So whose party is it?'

'Oh, so you *are* interested.'

'Of course I'm interested!'

'It's a very old friend of mine—we grew up together. His family also own one of La Rioja's finest vineyards.'

'And does their wine rival the de la Camara vines?' she teased.

'What do you think?' he drawled.

Well, *let* him be in a bad mood, she thought defiantly. She certainly wasn't going to pander to it! He should be purring with delight—not grouchy like this. She remembered in breathtaking detail what had just happened on the sofa, but his attitude dampened the afterglow of their erotic encounter.

'I think you should wipe that frown from your face!' she said crossly.

And he would like to wipe that furious little look from *her* face with his lips, but by now they were sweeping up the drive with another car close behind them.

Outside, there were brightly coloured lanterns illuminating the house in rainbow-coloured hues, and when they stepped out into the warm night air they could hear the sound of music and laughter coming from the direction of the swimming pool.

'Ready?' he questioned, and held his arm out for her to link it, but Sophie ignored it. She was certainly not going to appear on his arm looking like some kind of *trophy!*

'Let's go,' she said instead.

He introduced her to Laurent Gomez, their host, and his beautiful pregnant wife, Maria.

'What will you drink, Sophie?' Maria asked, with a genuinely welcoming smile on her face.

Sophie relaxed. 'Some wine, please.'

'You will try some Spanish champagne?' asked Laurent. 'Though strictly speaking we are not allowed to call it that, for our French rivals have the monopoly on the name—but I can assure you that you will find it just as delicious.'

'Sounds lovely,' said Sophie, and glanced up at Luis, but his face was unsmiling as he met her eyes. What was *wrong* with him this evening? 'When is your baby due?' she asked Maria.

'In time for Navidad—Christmas,' dimpled Maria.

'And it is your first?'

'My fifth!'

'Good heavens,' said Sophie weakly. 'You look about the same age as me!'

'She is,' commented Luis drily. 'Just that some women start young and then never seem to stop, is that not so, Maria?'

'This is my last!' said Maria fervently.

'Last what?' enquired Laurent, who was returning with a tray of champagne.

'Nothing, *querido,*' murmured his wife, and winked at Sophie.

Sophie began to relax even more. Luis's friends were charming and they seemed to accept her—the close friends, in any case. As usual she was aware of the more quizzical looks from the unattached females, but she didn't really care. They could ogle him as much as they liked—*she* was the one who was with him!

After two glasses of delicious champagne, all she cared about was why Luis seemed so stern and so solemn, but she didn't get an opportunity to ask him, since they were never alone.

She had just been given a plate of paella, and was preparing to go and find Luis, to eat with him, when Sophie became aware of a split-second silence, followed by an unmistakable buzz of excitement. She looked up to see what or who had caused it.

It was a woman of such outstanding beauty that for a moment Sophie was certain that she had seen her on the front of a glossy magazine. And maybe she had.

She was tall—almost as tall as the tallest man at the party, who, naturally, just happened to be Luis. Her silver dress clung like a mermaid's tail to every slim curve of her show-stopping body and her thick dark hair was piled high on her head in an elaborate confection of curls, studded with jewels which glittered so brightly that they might very well have been real diamonds.

But it was her face which was the most extraordinary thing about her, and it seemed to personify all that was magnificent about Spanish women. An oval face, with enormous black eyes and a soft, luscious mouth painted red. A face which contained passion as well as beauty.

'Who's that?' whispered Sophie.

There was a slight, awkward pause. 'That is

Alejandra,' replied Maria carefully. 'Have you not yet met?'

No, of course they had not met—for why on earth would Luis introduce his current mistress to his former one? Wouldn't that put him in a more than precarious position if, say, the two women began comparing notes?

And what would she hear? Sophie wondered painfully. Would Alejandra describe a relationship just like the one she was currently enjoying with Luis?

Maybe it was time to stop deluding herself that what they had between them was something special. Luis treated her with respect, yes, and maybe their affair would continue for longer than his previous one, but that was only because she had ensured a secure position in his life by offering to care for his son.

'No,' she said slowly, and put the plate of untouched food back down on the table. 'We haven't met. Excuse me, please, Maria, I must go and find Luis.'

But Luis was nowhere to be found, and in the end Sophie grabbed a glass of fruit juice and went over to a shaded corner of the pool, unable to face anyone or make anything which would pass as conversation.

She sat down on a lounger, and gave a long, heavy sigh. She was either going to have to toughen up or get out while she still had the strength to do so. She had said that she would reassess after a year, but tonight her insecurity was threatening to swamp her. They had been happy these three months, yes—but he had been happy with Miranda once. And Alejandra, too. So was it going to happen all over again? Would Luis tire of her once the lust had burnt itself out?

The sound of a footstep disturbed her troubled thoughts and she looked up to see Alejandra standing there, looking like a shining, ethereal moonbeam in her clinging silver dress.

'You must be Sophie,' said Alejandra in perfect, accentless English which held a faint transatlantic drawl. 'Do you know who I am?'

'Of course,' said Sophie staunchly, but the hand that put the glass down onto the table beside her was shaking. 'You're Alejandra.'

Alejandra didn't say anything for a moment, just studied her without embarrassment. Then she said, almost ruefully, 'You are very beautiful.'

'And so are you.'

'He likes blondes,' said Alejandra reflectively. 'He always has done.'

She made her feel like one in a long production line of blondes, thought Sophie indignantly! But maybe she was. She opened her mouth to utter some meaningless platitude to the woman who had shared Luis's bed for who knew how long, when a dark figure appeared out of the shadows and the tall Spaniard stood there, as still as if he had been carved from stone.

His eyes were watchful, but that was all she could read in them in this dim evening light.

'Ah, so you two have met.'

The master of understatement, thought Sophie, and she gave him a cool look.

Alejandra took a step forward, her cheek held towards him for a kiss, but to Sophie's surprise he merely inclined his head in a more formal greeting. 'Alejandra,' he said calmly. 'You are looking well.'

'And you, too, *querido,*' she murmured, but her mouth curved in a swift, almost painful smile, as if she acknowledged the bitter fact that something fundamental in their relationship had changed. 'Domesticity clearly suits you.'

Was that designed to ruffle him? Sophie wondered. To make it sound as though the latest blonde had him in her clutches?

'Indeed it does,' he agreed, and looked at Sophie. 'You have eaten, *querida?*'

As if food would have done anything but choke her! 'I'm not very hungry,' she said truthfully.

'Then you would like to dance?'

'Actually, Luis, what I would like most is to go home. I hate to be a party-pooper, but I'm really very tired!'

'Ask Laurent's driver to run you home,' suggested Alejandra, imperceptibly drawing her splendid shoulders back so that the full impact of her breasts could be seen through the stretched silver fabric.

'I'm tired myself,' said Luis blandly, though his eyes glittered a secret, shining message to Sophie. 'Come along, Sophie—let's get your shawl and go home. Goodnight, Alejandra.' Once again he inclined his head with faultless courtesy. 'It's good to see you again.'

'Goodnight,' she answered tonelessly.

Sophie didn't say a word until they were back on the road to the hacienda, and then it all came spilling out of her mouth like poison.

'You *knew* she was going to be there, didn't you?' she accused.

'Of course I knew.'

'But you didn't see fit to tell me?'

'You didn't ask.'

'So what if I didn't ask? You should have realised that I would have wanted to know!'

'I didn't think you'd care,' he commented drily.

But Sophie was too caught up in her own rage to analyse the meaning of his words. 'I would never have gone if I'd known she was going to be there!'

'Why ever not?'

'Oh, don't be so naïve, Luis!' she said furiously. 'Don't you think that everyone must have been sniggering into their drinks to see your past and your current mistress together at the same party? Was that your intention? To humiliate me?'

He swore softly in Spanish as the car bumped down the drive towards the hacienda. 'You think that?' he demanded. 'You honestly think that?'

'What else am I supposed to think?'

'I offered you my arm on our arrival,' he accused, 'to show the world that you are the woman in my life, but you refused it, didn't you? Cool, cold Sophie and her don't-touch-me quality which would freeze water on the hottest day!'

'I'm not staying around to listen while you insult me!'

She jumped out of the car door and slammed it, marching straight into the house and storming into the sitting room with Luis hot on her heels. Once the door was closed behind him and they were alone she turned on him furiously.

'You were trying to make me jealous, weren't you, Luis?'

There was a long pause, and then he nodded. '*Sì*. Maybe I was.'

She stared at him. 'Why would you want to make me jealous?'

He gave a short laugh. 'Now who's being the naïve one?'

'I don't—I don't understand.'

And suddenly everything which had been bubbling away inside him for weeks now came to a violent boil. 'Don't you?' he demanded. 'Don't you really? I suppose that I must be grateful that you *do* appear jealous—at least that shows me you feel *something* for me!'

'Luis—'

'Do you have any idea what it is like to be made to feel nothing more than a stud?' he stormed.

'A *stud?*'

'A man who pleases you in bed, but is fit for nothing more!'

'Luis, that is ridiculous,' she protested. 'We do all kind of things together; you know we do.'

'I know that you do them while keeping me at arm's length, with those witchy blue eyes and that cool, mocking smile! But the only time I feel close to you is when I am making love to you.' He gave a snort of derision. 'And you wonder why I say that I feel like a stud!'

She had never seen him so het-up before, nor quite so *Spanish,* and she realised that for all his aristocratic upbringing and his fluent English, this man who stood before her now was a living, breathing Latin, with all the passion and the turbulence which went along with his heritage. But her confusion was genuine as her anger began to seep away, replaced by a desperate need to know what she should have asked him a long time ago. 'What is it that you want from me, Luis?'

Black fire sparked from his eyes. 'Nothing that you are not prepared to give,' he answered proudly.

And suddenly the thought that she might lose him became horribly and frighteningly real. 'I...thought that I was a good mistress,' she said haltingly.

Again he swore in Spanish. 'And you are! The very best mistress in the world!' he raged, and his eyes lanced into her as though they were black lasers. 'But I do not want a mistress! Not any more.'

Her mouth fell open and her heart began beating with distress as she bit out the painful words. 'You mean...you mean you want me to go away?'

'Madre de Dios! Must I spell it out for you in words of one syllable? I want to know what goes on in that mad, crazy, cool English heart of yours! No, I do not want you to go away—I want to know how you *feel!'*

'About what?'

His eyes blazed. 'About what?' he demanded incredulously. 'About *me,* of course!'

She turned away. He wanted too much! He wanted it all, and more besides.

'Sophie?' he said, on a note which came as close as Luis ever would to pleading.

'No,' she said stubbornly.

He looked at the defiant set of her shoulders. 'Why not?' he asked quietly.

'Because feelings were not part of the deal! I came here on the understanding that I would look after your

son and share your bed. That was the agreement—
your words, Luis, not mine.'

'And what if I told you that I was no longer content
with the present agreement?'

She turned around. 'Just what are you getting at?'

'That feelings change, or maybe I was just too
blind to see that they had been there all along. You
see—' He bit his lip, as if trying to work out how to
say words which were foreign to him. 'I love you,
Sophie. I love you with all my heart—'

'But you don't know what love is,' she protested
weakly, though her own heart was beating fit to burst.
'Remember?'

'How could I ever forget?' he said bitterly, wondering if he had been half-crazy himself to have ever
said such a thing. But she was still standing an arm's
length away, and her eyes were still wary and uncon-
vinced. He struggled to put his own feelings into
words, something which really *was* foreign to him.

'What would you say if I told you that I think I
fell in love with you the moment I saw you? Sophie,
it was a feeling so strong that it rocked the very foun-
dations of my world—'

'Please don't!' she interrupted before he could say
any more. 'That was wrong—you know it was! You
were due to be married *to my cousin!*'

'You cannot help the way that someone makes you
feel,' he argued sombrely. 'It is what you *do* about
those feelings which makes it right or wrong. And I
did nothing. Nothing at all. And neither did you.'

'I wanted you, too,' she whispered. 'And I felt so
guilty about it. That's why I taught myself to hate
you, to convince myself that you were looking at

every other woman the way you looked at me that day.'

He shook his head. 'Never,' he said softly. 'I have never looked at another woman in such a way, but then no other woman makes me feel the way you do, Sophie. Women have plotted and schemed and made demands on me, but not you—and you see, I have grown to love you very much, and I still don't know how you feel about me.'

Sophie suddenly felt as though she had drunk a glass of champagne too quickly. 'Luis,' she said weakly. 'Will you hold me? Please?'

He needed no second bidding, just reached out and pulled her against him, his strong arms supporting her, protecting her. He closed his eyes and rested his cheek against the silk of her hair.

'Anyway, you do know,' she said indistinctly against his chest.

He lifted her chin, both moved and disturbed to see the tears which glittered in her blue eyes. 'Do I, *querida* mine?'

'Yes,' she sniffed. 'You must do. Of course I love you! You must be used to women falling in love with you all the time.'

Diplomatically he ignored that. 'You didn't act like you loved me,' he mused instead. 'Emotionally you kept me at a distance, Sophie; you cannot deny that.'

'Because love makes you vulnerable, that's why.'

'Don't I just know it?' he commented drily.

She stared at him as if he had just told her that the sun would shine at night. 'You? Vulnerable? Never!'

'Yes, sometimes. With you.' He smiled. 'You see,

with you it's different—different from anything I have ever experienced, or expected to.'

But the past came thudding down, like a dark and heavy thundercloud, and all Sophie's fears came spilling out. 'I can't stay with you, Luis—'

He stilled. 'Not *stay* with me?' he repeated incredulously.

She shook her head, knowing that she must confront her fears head-on, not leave them festering beneath the surface, where they could eat into her confidence and her life.

She shook her head. 'Not if I thought you were ever going to take another mistress—*ever,*' she emphasised fiercely, and turned her blue eyes up to him. 'And how do I know you won't?'

'Because I make that vow to you,' he said softly. 'Never, ever, ever—and have I ever lied to you, Sophie?'

She shook her head.

'How can I look at any woman ever again?' he said simply. 'Do you not know that you hold my heart in the palm of your hand, Sophie?'

It was the most wonderful thing anyone had ever said to her. A tear began to track its way down her cheek, and he made a reprimanding little sound as he wiped it away with his lips. 'Ssh,' he soothed. 'No more tears. No need for any tears. Come, Sophie, come and sit beside me over here.'

He led her to the window-seat and sat her down as tenderly as if she were a child, then raised her hand to his lips and kissed the fingertips thoughtfully.

'When did it happen?' she asked, loving this new reverence and homage. 'When did you know?'

He shrugged. 'Who knows? When you went back to England I missed you like crazy, and at first I tried to tell myself that it was just frustration. But frustration does not usually eat into your very soul. I wanted you,' he said simply. 'Here. With me. Always.'

'You took long enough to come and ask me,' she complained.

He nodded. 'But of course—because I needed to be sure. Because what I was asking of you was a big thing, *querida*. I could not risk Teo's happiness if I thought it would not work out, that you would have to leave him again. And anyway—' he gave her a rueful look '—I did not know what your answer would be. How did I know that you would agree to give up your high-powered life in England to come and live with me? It was my wildest, sweetest wish come true.'

Now feeling more than a little content, she also felt secure enough to bat him a look from between slitted lashes. 'And what if I had not agreed?'

'Then I would have come to get you,' he said darkly. 'Some way. Somehow. I knew I would have you in the end.'

Sophie shivered, thinking that she rather liked the sound of that. 'And now?'

The kiss to her fingertips became a little nip, and then a voluptuous lick of his tongue, and he smiled, seeing her pupils dilate in response. 'Now we go to bed, *querida,* and we make beautiful love together—'

'No change there, then?'

'And then you will tell me exactly when you will agree to marry me.'

EPILOGUE

SHE kept him waiting for almost a year, until Luis was almost climbing the walls. He had thought that he had felt frustration when she was far away from him in England but he had been wrong. This, he thought distractedly, *this* was frustration!

Did she expect him to beg? Because if so she was in for a big disappointment—for, although she had captured his heart for more than a lifetime, a de la Camara would never *beg!*

But he asked her to be his wife from time to time, usually when he found her especially irresistible, and her answer was always the same.

'Not yet, Luis. Not yet.'

'Why do you make me wait, *querida* mine?' he growled.

She touched her fingertips to his mouth. 'Because it isn't the right time.'

'When, then?'

'You'll be the first to know,' she whispered, and kissed him. 'And it's probably the first time you've ever had to wait for anything in your life!'

This much was true. Life's pleasures and rewards had always dropped with astonishing ease into the lap of Luis de la Camara and he was discovering for himself that delayed gratification could be a potent aphrodisiac! Sophie had laughed when he told her *that.*

'As if *you* had any need of an aphrodisiac!' she gurgled.

She was now learning Spanish and Luis arranged to have a tutor visit each afternoon while Teo had his nap. She took her studies seriously—so seriously, in fact, that Luis had wondered aloud if she would end up with a larger vocabulary than him!

'Very probably,' she said serenely.

And Teo had grown from a plump baby into the most enchanting toddler, who now called Sophie ''Mama''. The first time he said it she had felt her eyes filling with tears and had looked over at Luis and seen the responding telltale glitter in his own.

'It would be nice to give Teo a brother or a sister one of these days,' he commented in bed that night.

Sophie was still basking in the aftermath of an earth-shattering orgasm. 'Would it?'

'Mmm.' He leaned back over her and trickled a finger down to where she was still wet and pulsing with him, and she shuddered. 'We could have a lot of fun together, making babies, Soph-ie.'

'We have a lot of fun together now,' she protested weakly, but then he started kissing her, and she was lost.

Then one day, in his study, she put the phone down and turned to him expectantly.

'My parents want to come and stay,' she announced.

He looked up from his paperwork. 'So I gathered. I'm delighted,' he murmured. 'When?'

'Late next week.'

He nodded. 'I'll clear my diary.'

Luis had met her parents twice, when he had taken

Sophie back to England with Teo, and once he had
dispelled their initial wariness with his obvious love
for their daughter they began to think him the greatest
thing since sliced bread.

They had visited her grandmother, too, and her
London-based friends, and even Liam had grudgingly
begun to accept that the aristocratic Spaniard made
her happy.

'Darling Luis,' she murmured.

He feasted his black eyes on her extravagantly.
'Mmm?'

'You know my parents are coming out?'

'Well, since you told me that just moments ago,
yes, I do, *querida,*' he commented drily. 'My memory
is not quite that defective!'

'Well…' She drew a deep breath, knowing that she
had put the moment off for as long as it needed to
be. Miranda's memory would not be sullied, nor
would any of their families feel any emotion other
than happiness for them. 'It sort of seems a pity not
to make the most of it,' she said slowly.

'You want me to throw a party for them?'

'*Us* to throw a party,' she corrected. 'Yes, I do.'
She looked at him from between slitted lashes. 'We
could make it a wedding party, if you like.'

He gave a lazy smile. 'Come over here.'

She did as he asked, went and sat on his knee and
put her arms tightly around his neck.

'You're going to marry me at last, are you,
Sophie?'

'Yes, please!'

'And you're quite sure?'

She gazed down at the black eyes which glittered

at her with such love and longing that a lump rose in her throat, and it was a moment before she could speak. 'Oh, yes, my beloved Don Luis,' she whispered. 'I've never been more sure of anything in my life.'

Modern Romance™
...seduction and
passion guaranteed

Tender Romance™
...love affairs that
last a lifetime

Sensual Romance™
...sassy, sexy and
seductive

Blaze
...sultry days and
steamy nights

Medical Romance™
...medical drama on
the pulse

Historical Romance™
...rich, vivid and
passionate

27 new titles every month.

*With all kinds of Romance for
every kind of mood...*

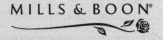

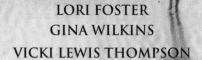

Do you think you can write a Mills & Boon novel?

Then this is your chance!

We're looking for sensational new authors to write for the Modern Romance™ series!

Could you transport readers into a world of provocative, tantalizing romantic excitement? These compelling modern fantasies capture the drama and intensity of a powerful, sensual love affair. The stories portray spirited, independent heroines and irresistible heroes in international settings. The conflict between these characters should be balanced by a developing romance that may include explicit lovemaking.

What should you do next?

To submit a manuscript [complete manuscript 55,000 words]
OR
For more information on writing novels for Modern Romance™

Please write to :-
Editorial Department, Harlequin Mills & Boon Ltd, Eton House, 18-24 Paradise Road, Richmond, Surrey, TW9 1SR or visit our website at **www.millsandboon.co.uk**

Modern Romance…
"seduction and passion guaranteed"

Submissions to:
Harlequin Mills & Boon Editorial Department,
Eton House, 18-24 Paradise Road, Richmond, Surrey, TW9 1SR,
United Kingdom.

2FREE
books and a surprise gift!

We would like to take this opportunity to thank you for reading this Mills & Boon® book by offering you the chance to take TWO more specially selected titles from the Modern Romance™ series absolutely FREE! We're also making this offer to introduce you to the benefits of the Reader Service™—

★ FREE home delivery
★ FREE gifts and competitions
★ FREE monthly Newsletter
★ Exclusive Reader Service discount
★ Books available before they're in the shops

Accepting these FREE books and gift places you under no obligation to buy, you may cancel at any time, even after receiving your free shipment. Simply complete your details below and return the entire page to the address below. *You don't even need a stamp!*

YES! Please send me 2 free Modern Romance books and a surprise gift. I understand that unless you hear from me, I will receive 4 superb new titles every month for just £2.55 each, postage and packing free. I am under no obligation to purchase any books and may cancel my subscription at any time. The free books and gift will be mine to keep in any case.

P2ZEA

Ms/Mrs/Miss/Mr ....Initials....................................
                                                    BLOCK CAPITALS PLEASE
Surname ....
Address ....

....
....Postcode................................

Send this whole page to:
UK: FREEPOST CN81, Croydon, CR9 3WZ
EIRE: PO Box 4546, Kilcock, County Kildare (stamp required)